BETTIE PAGE

BETTIE PAGE

Aphrodite Rising

KIMBERLY US

To my husband, Steve—
Thank you for your endless support

Contents

I

Greetings from Mt. Olympus

It may surprise you, but the Greek Gods and Goddesses are still around and amusing ourselves with your earthly lives. Despite the newer religions, people can still feel us acting upon them or through them. Psychology replaced the word *God/Goddess* with *archetype*, which is defined as powerful inner forces. New name, but it's really me and my family entertaining ourselves through you mortals.

Every woman has goddess-given talents that act within her. The key to an authentic life, one lived from the soul, is to recognize the gifts of her goddess and use them. Too often, women feel their inner goddess and repress her out of fear of attracting criticism. Many Athenas never own their intelligence and power and, instead, choose to support a powerful man. Plenty of Artemis women are afraid of their fierce independence and love of nature, and choose a safe life lived indoors, instead of a life of exploration.

I'm Aphrodite, the Goddess of Love, Beauty, Sex and Passion. I am a challenging archetype to possess. It breaks my heart how many of you repress me instead of enjoying a life of flirtation, attractiveness and great sex. My voice gets silenced through the warnings of parents and the shaming of peers and society.

You can spot women who welcome my archetype because we radiate a magnetic attractiveness that pulls men towards us. We are witty conversationalists and happy flirts, but our secret weapon is our attentiveness. An Aphrodite woman listens to a man with her ears and her body. The focus of her attention makes him feel like he is the only person in the world and the most handsome.

We love our bodies and, even when they aren't classically perfect, we delight in them and feel confident. This is a true gift in a society that makes money off of telling women they are too fat and our natural body odors are something to be masked. An Aphrodite woman knows her worth and knows she is beautiful.

Despite our considerable gifts, the life of an Aphrodite isn't always easy. We attract sexual attention even when we don't seek it. Women, particularly Hera types, hate us and our charm can make others feel insecure or jealous. We live in the moment and love sex, so we tend to leave a string of broken hearts behind us. The hardest part of an Aphrodite life is the patriarchy frowns upon a sexually liberated woman, and they pull out their entire arsenal to try and put us in our place and make us behave.

My goal is to end the patriarchy's control over sex. My motto is "my sexuality belongs to me." I want to create a society that honors women, gives them control over their bodies, and allows them to express themselves freely. Sex expresses passion, and passion is truth. Sex is beautiful and not something to be shamed.

Judgement and shame are the tools the patriarchy uses to keep women under their control, and I want to steal those tools and throw them into Hades. I don't want a matriarchy. I dream of a society of equals living in beauty, laughter, and openness.

When I find an earthly woman who possesses my archetype, and has the skills to help me accomplish my goals, I will inhabit her body as that voice she hears in her brain. Some people call it intuition, or soul—whatever the term—you know what I'm talking about.

Maybe you have even noticed that the voice in your head doesn't always sound like you? Have you argued with it? Have you noticed that sometimes the voice is wiser, or edgier, or more cautious than your regular self? This usually indicates that I, or one of my relatives, is in residence.

Homer explained how we operate in *The Iliad* and *The Odyssey*. But since that time, Zeus has put some new rules in place. We are no longer allowed to appear before mortals, or take direct actions as ourselves.

Gods and goddesses can only act by entering a mortal that already has their archetype, and is capable of living in a way that embodies us. When that happens, the spirit of the goddess can have a body experience through the mortal. We turn up the volume of your authentic self and make it harder for you to repress your true nature, but we can't force you to do anything you don't want to do.

The truth is that most women have several goddess archetypes inside of them. Two of us may have our eye on the same woman, so the rivalry between the goddesses continues. However, we have sworn off offering mortals bribes because of the fiasco we created fighting over that apple.

What apple, you ask? Allow me to refresh your memory. Thetis, a beautiful sea nymph, was marrying King Peleus. Her wedding was the event of the eon and everyone buzzed in anticipation of it. However, there was one goddess who did not receive an invitation: Eris, the Goddess of Discord and mother of the Spirit of Strife. With a title like that, it isn't hard to imagine why the bride wanted her left off the guest list.

The wedding was a lovely affair. Thetis' colors were iridescent and pink. Bubbles floated in the air. We ate ambrosia off of scallop shells, and the scent of jasmine wafted through the hall. Apollo played his lyre. Hermes accompanied him on a shepherd-pipe, and the muses sang. The guests had outdone themselves and looked gorgeous. I wore a violet tunic embroidered with doves, which was secured with my filigreed girdle and a broach embedded with abalone shells. A veil, decorated with tiny pearls, covered my long, curled hair.

Hera and Athena looked fabulous as well. We were standing together, and I had just complimented Hera's amber necklace, when Eris appeared. She looked unkempt, as usual. Her hair was greasy and matted, her tunic mud-stained, and her eyes ablaze with fury. She stood at the door, cackled, and tossed a golden apple, inscribed with "For the Fairest," into the reception hall.

Hera, Athena, and I instantly dove for it. In a most unladylike pile, we wrestled for control of it, each of us certain of our superior beauty. Zeus commanded us to stop and, in unison, we said, "As King of the Gods, we ask you to decide to whom the apple belongs."

That wily fellow deferred, and he told us, "Go ask Paris. He is a mortal with an eye for beautiful women." He looked over at Poseidon, and the pair high-fived and laughed.

We left the reception at once and found Paris living as a shepherd. The nymph that accompanied us handed him the apple and said, "Zeus decrees that you decide which of these goddesses is the fairest."

Paris looked over each of us like prized heifers. His eyes scanned us head to toe, impertinently lingering on our breasts and hips. He had us walk an imaginary runway and do a model twirl at the end. Needless to say, the three of us were getting annoyed with him, but were too proud to walk away without the apple. Paris dragged out making his judgement, so we began offering him bribes. Hera promised him power over all the kingdoms of Asia; Athena offered him victory in all his battles; and I offered him the most beautiful woman in the world. Paris instantly handed the apple to me.

Believe me, I had no intention of starting the Trojan War. I didn't think Helen of Sparta was the most beautiful woman in the world. In fact, when I made the offer, I thought Paris would choose Arketa, a lovely single maiden living on Mt. Ida. However, it turned out that Paris wasn't a mere shepherd—he was a prince of Troy. He saw Helen, the wife of King Menelaus, on a diplomatic mission. He abducted her, and war broke out. Hera and Athena, along with Poseidon, Hermes, and Hephaestus, sided with the Greeks. Apollo, Artemis, Ares and I sided with the Trojans. Eventually, my side lost.

Everyone blames me for starting that war but, in my defense, it was Hera that made things so awful. She hated Paris for not picking her as the fairest and would not rest until all of Troy was destroyed.

After the Trojan War, Zeus called Hera, Athena, and me before him. He lectured us like a high school principal on our poor choices and the consequences. At the end of the disciplinary meeting, he decreed that we had to play nice. We had to be less antagonistic towards each other in our mortal meddling. Hera, Athena, and I have mostly buried the hatchet, with the exception of a few long-standing grudges.

Generally, Athena and I let Hera have who she wants because she focuses on jealous, wronged women. She derives great delight in entering them to help craft revenge against their spouses. I'm sure you have seen her work. Her women usually earn nicknames such as "Black Widow" or "Cannibal Kathy."

Unfortunately, Athena and I have the same type. We both like intelligent, strong women. Native intelligence gives us so much more to work with. Tough, resilient women, who refuse to play the victim, are more fun. Cleopatra, was my work, as was Theodora, wife of Emperor Justinian I. Athena's famous products included scientist Marie Curie, and the Queen of Sheba.

Sometimes both of us will want the same mortal. When this happens, Zeus mandated that we have to let the mortal "choose" which goddess she is most like through her actions. Until she does a decisive action, we can only watch her, waiting for the perfect moment to enter.

It is no surprise that we both had our eye on Bettie Page.

At first glance, Bettie was pure Athena: straight A student, regimental sponsor for the ROTC, secretary-treasurer for the Student Council, co-editor of both the school newspaper and the yearbook. Her classmates voted her "Most Likely to Succeed." She was a virgin and barely flirted with boys. She never drank or smoked. Bettie was such a good girl it made me nauseous.

So why didn't I just leave her to Athena? Bettie had "it." She never looked at the boys, but they couldn't take their eyes off of her. She had such natural charm and friendliness that they found her irresistible. Her amazing figure, with a tiny waist and curvy breasts and hips, sealed the deal. I knew she was an Aphrodite inside because she adored acting. She did her other extra-curriculars out of duty and ambition, but she came alive as the star of school plays. She was the program director of the Dramatics Club and intuitively selected plays that showcased her vivaciousness.

In Bettie, I could see a woman that would have the strength to embody me, Aphrodite. Her intelligence and work ethic would put her in a position that would allow me to challenge the double-standards of the patriarchy. Her charm and friendliness would keep her from getting dismissed as a slut and offer a different image of a sexual female.

Athena, of course, argued with me. "I hate to see a girl like that only accomplish your sexual goals. With me inside of her, she could run for office. We could change the power structure from the top down."

"Your work through Susan B. Anthony won women the right to vote, but they are still asking their husbands to make their choices. We need to tackle the patriarchy from a different angle."

"Through sex? That is the only role they want us to occupy. You are sending us backwards."

"Athena, you don't understand men. You don't even like them. You're a virgin goddess."

"So what? Look what caring about men has done for Hera, Demeter, and Persephone. No, it is better to keep our distance from men. You could learn from Hestia, Artemis and myself. As virgins, we are truly independent," said Athena.

"Females can't change society by rejecting men. We have to transform them."

"And how do you do that?" demanded Athena.

"By seducing them. For a powerless woman, the first trick is seduction. Draw men to you, and then they might listen and change their mind. Prove their stereotypes wrong. If we are ever going to have control over our bodies, we must eliminate the double standard that sex belongs to men and is something done to women. We need to show that women crave it too. That will be our next step towards equality."

Athena grunted a dismissal of my argument. "Good thing Zeus decreed the mortal gets to decide. All we can do is watch Bettie and see which one of us wins her."

"May the best goddess win."

2

Skippin' Class

"I'm just not getting my lines straight," Bettie said to her best friend, Nora. "Max agreed to read lines with me today, but he wants me to ditch third period to do it."

The pair sat in the cafeteria of Hume-Fogg High School. Bettie had already wolfed down her spaghetti, and I knew it was the only hot meal she would eat that day. She tried to keep her eyes off of Nora's plate and bounced her fork on the table by pressing on the metal tines.

"Ditch Mrs. Stark's class? Are you crazy?" Nora made a circle in the air near her temple.

"Uggh, I know. She barely likes me as it is—" *Tap. Tap. Tap* went the fork.

Exasperated, Nora grabbed it away from Bettie. She opened her milk carton. "That's because she's jealous. The way her husband fawned all over you at the Scrap Collection—the poor woman."

"He's exactly like my Dad. It didn't matter where he was—church, the movies—any time, any place. My Dad would hone in on other women like a tom-cat in heat. It made my mom crazy, and they'd yell and fight all night."

Bettie stiffened with annoyance as Bubba sat down at the table beside her.

"Hi Bettie," he grinned at her, but she looked away, "and Nora." Bettie's friend gave him an encouraging smile.

"Hi Bubba, are you going to the play next weekend?" He started to shake his head. Nora added, "Bettie's the star."

"Well, then I guess I'll have to go see some hoity-toity Shake-speare and support you." Bettie still wouldn't give him eye contact so, with a wink at Nora, he left the table.

"Why do you have to be so rude? He's so cute," scolded Nora.

"I'm not interested. If Bubba would spend half as much time paying attention to the teacher, instead of always looking over his shoulder at me, then he might have a chance of passing math." Bettie shrugged. "As it is, it looks like he's going to have to do his senior year over."

Nora blew a raspberry. "You're lucky you are my friend. It makes me so jealous the way every guy pays attention to you."

"It is not that great––believe me. Look at the trouble it got me into with Mrs. Stark. It's not like I did anything to encourage that old goat." The girls put their book satchels over their arm and stood up with their trays. They walked to the service window, placed their silverware in the bin, and slid their empty trays towards the old lady who did the dishes.

"So about ditching Mrs. Stark's class," she stopped Nora with a hand on her arm. "I don't want to be an artist, so maybe it doesn't matter—right?" Bettie asked.

"Well, I wouldn't do it. But when have you ever listened to me?" Nora playfully bumped Bettie's shoulder with hers as they walked into the hallway.

"One class shouldn't matter. I do all my work and always get A's.

Besides, I can't flub up my lines again at practice. Mr. Price already threatened to take the lead away and give it to my understudy. Imagine Suzie as Lady Macbeth."

"The Scottish Play would certainly suffer for it." Nora pantomimed washing her hands, as she imitated the nasal tone of Suzie, "Out, Out, damn spot."

Bettie laughed. "That settles it." She made a grand sweep with her hand. "I must skip Art for the good of the Theater."

"Break a leg," said Nora as the bell rang, and the girls went their separate ways.

#

Athena and I looked at each other. I was grinning like a cat with a canary, or should I say the cat that caught an owl, because one look at Athena's pursed lips told me she was taking this personally and somehow blaming me.

Athena shook her head. "What is she thinking? All four years, she has been aiming for class valedictorian. No matter what sacrifices she had to make, she stayed focused. And now? Skipping that harridan's class? It doesn't take a deity to predict the future. Mrs. Stark is full of Hera—she'll find a way to avenge her husband's wandering eye."

I laughed and winked. "I'm going to get this girl and there isn't even a man involved. I'm not used to victories like this. She's letting her true nature show by breaking the rules. Oh, and she's so smart and driven—this is going to be delightful."

"She said she was ditching to practice with Max—is there a man involved?" Athena asked. I smiled to myself thinking that Athena was so immune to men that she didn't even realize Max was gay. In the closet of course, no one would dare be out in those days, but still--drama, voice, affectation. Max wasn't using his acting skills to hide his true nature.

"No, I promise you. She isn't ditching for Max," I said. "She just isn't your girl, Athena. Seems like theater and being the center of attention is more important than knowledge."

#

When Athena said Mrs. Stark was full of Hera, she meant it literally. It often happens that, when one of us targets a human of interest, the other gods and goddesses come to see what the excitement is about. It was natural, with both Athena and I eyeing Bettie, that Hera would start snooping around.

It didn't take her long to find a disaffected wife. It's pretty sad how many of those are out there. The sacred institution of marriage seems doomed to fail––the binding marital contract, the demand to "look only at me," and the expectation that one person can meet all sexual and companionship needs. How does Hera, Goddess of Matrimony, really think that can work?

To be fair, Hera never wanted to get married. She wanted to remain a virgin goddess, like Athena and Artemis, but Zeus looked into her huge, long-lashed, cow-eyes and knew he had to have her. He tried the traditional courting and complimenting route, but Hera was immune to his charms. So, Zeus used his other charms to trick her.

Hera loves animals. In the human world, I smile when a little girl races up to every dog she sees to pet it, or when the older woman lives a life with her cats. Those females have Hera in them. Zeus knew her weakness, of course, and exploited it. He transformed himself into a fledgling cuckoo bird and stood out in the rain, shaking and shivering with his little grey feathers matted and dripping. Hera took one look and picked up the sweet baby bird and held it to her magnificent breasts to warm it.

Zeus transformed himself back into a man and, before she could push him away, raped her. Ashamed and feeling ruined, Hera agreed to marry Zeus to earn her respect back. Poor thing. Zeus truly does love her, but he is the most alpha of all males, so her expectation of fidelity was folly. It didn't take long for Zeus to start slipping out of Mt. Olympus and sampling the mortals and nymphs of earth. As the Goddess of Marriage, she would never consider having an affair herself, so she is trapped by the institution she represents and suffers the rage of a woman scorned.

Needless to say, the humans on Earth who idealize marriage often find themselves in similar situations. It is tragic how many opportunities Hera has to enter a mortal compared to Athena, Artemis, or myself.

The rules for inhabiting mortals as set down by Zeus is that we can't take over their lives. We can enter at a turning point that they created by their free will. We can stay until they die unless their free will starts to reject our archetype. At that point, we need to voluntarily vacate their body and allow them to live out the remainder of their lives without us.

Bettie's decision to ditch Mrs. Stark's class was the beginning of her turning point, but I couldn't enter her yet. As part of the decree that the goddesses "play nice," we are not allowed to get into conflicts with each other while inhabiting mortals. Things escalate too quickly when omnipotent egos are involved. Knowing that Bettie had an upcoming confrontation with Hera/Mrs. Stark, I was more than willing to wait.

#

The next day, a thunderstorm raged, boding ill. Bettie came into art class with a friendly smile and sat down, playing the role of a perfect student. Mrs. Stark pointedly did not look at her or call on her, even when she raised her hand to participate.

As the period dragged on, Bettie grew uncertain and dread began to fill her. Her gaze darted around the room for something to distract her thoughts. Portraits of George Washington and Franklin Roosevelt hung on the wall. She gazed at Roosevelt's calming image, but jumped when a lightning bolt flashed, followed immediately by a clap of thunder that sounded like an explosion. "The only thing we have to fear is fear itself," she mumbled.

I studied Mrs. Stark and knew her type. She was frumpy and bore the look of a woman who had given up on herself. Her short hair clung to her head like a helmet. The reading glasses perched on the end of her nose were attached to her neck with a chain. Her flowered maroon dress hung to her mid-calf. Clearly designed for a belt, the waist of the dress clung tightly to her round belly, and her arms had floppy bat-wings, instead of triceps. On her feet were matronly black shoes. Their heels struck the linoleum-tiled floor sharply as she approached Bettie's desk.

"Miss Page, please stay after class," she said and walked away like a military general.

Bettie cringed. "Drat," she whispered under her breath and the students around her giggled.

"Suzie told her you were on campus and ditching her class," said Joe, the cute guy who sat next to her and had been trying, unsuccessfully, to catch Bettie's eye all year.

"Of course, she did." Bettie slumped in her chair and crossed her arms, but then she caught Mrs. Stark's reproving look. Bettie straightened her spine, pressed her knees together, and put her saddle shoes flat on the ground like a proper lady.

The class finally ended and Bettie waited until the students had left the room before she approached Mrs. Stark's desk. She noticed Joe lurking near the door, hoping to witness the confrontation.

"Yes, Mrs. Stark?" Bettie asked, her Southern drawl sounding syrupy sweet.

"Apparently you were on campus yesterday and decided that my class was unimportant?" The teacher said.

"Umm, yes. I mean no. Your class wasn't unimportant. It's just that I had to practice my lines. You see, I'm Lady Macbeth. Since it's such an important part, I needed more practice, and since I do all my work for you on time, and get A's, I thought…I thought…"

"You thought what?" Mrs. Stark put her hands on her hips and peered down through her spectacles at Bettie.

"I thought––I hoped it would be okay to miss one class." Bettie's voice trailed off as she finished.

"You thought it would be okay to miss MY class, because art isn't important—right? Not important like yearbook, or English, or math or DRAMA. It's just art so who cares?" Mrs. Stark turned away from Bettie and shuffled through the papers on her desk. She held up a ditto. Bettie read the title History and Craft of Weaving. "It appears that you missed our pop quiz. I made a new version of the test for you. You can spend this lunch hour getting caught up." Mrs. Stark gestured towards a seat in front of her desk and placed the test upon it. Bettie couldn't miss her triumphant smile.

Bettie stared at the first question: The set of vertical threads are known as the ___ and the set of horizontal threads are known as the ____.

She vaguely remembered Mrs. Stark spending one lesson on weaving. A lesson that Bettie had mostly tuned out as she ran through her lines in her head. Something about hand knotting, looms, and textile production—her memory was spotty.

"Warp and weft," Athena shouted. I jumped, not realizing she had been watching the scene unfold with me. "Weaving! I know this was Hera's idea, just to torment me. Hera knew no one could enter Bettie until she was finished confronting her. Hera must not realize that Bettie is yours, otherwise the test would be on the History of Make-Up."

I sighed and watched Bettie stumble through the questions. Holding her pencil loosely in sweaty hands, she wrote so lightly that her A, B, C pattern on the multiple choice looked like an apology. Her vague say-nothing answer for "Who was John Kay, and what important role did he play in the history of weaving?" sealed her fate. Bettie brushed away a tear, and I saw Mrs. Stark lick her thin lips. Trembling, Bettie brought her test up to the teacher who pulled out her red pen like a fencer preparing to duel.

"Wrong. Wrong. Wrong." The red pen slashed each question. "My goodness Bettie, I don't think I've ever had a student perform so poorly. Hmmm. What a shame. It looks like your mind has been truant for some time." With a flourish, Mrs. Stark wrote a giant F on the top of the page and handed the bloody paper to Bettie. "I trust you will attend every class for the remainder of the term." She dismissed her with a curt nod.

Joe waited outside in the hall. As Bettie rushed out, he put his hand on her arm to stop her and, without speaking, she handed him the test.

He whistled in dismay. "This isn't the same test we got—that one was a joke and easy peasy. Are your parents going to kill you?"

"My parents don't care about my grades. They don't even care if I attend school. But an F averaged with my grade, so late in the semester, I think it will drop me to a B." Bettie took the test back and stared at the F. A tear fell on the paper and the red ink ran.

"You're the perfect student. I figured you must have strict folks."

Bettie shook her head. "All that matters to my mom is that I clean the house and take care of my little brothers and sisters." She didn't add the fact that her mother, with only a third-grade education, had a huge chip on her shoulder towards school. She sneered at Bettie's scholastic ambitions.

"Well, a B isn't the end of the world, especially if your folks don't care. Man, you're lucky, my Dad would kill me if I got a B in an elective."

"You wouldn't have had to take that make-up test. Boys get sent to the principal for a whoop 'in as punishment for ditching. Instead, they had to be gentle because I'm a girl and make me kill my grade."

Joe ran his hand through his crew-cut. I could feel how he resisted the urge to touch Bettie. She looked so lovely and vulnerable standing there crying. Any man would want to swoop in and save her. But Bettie wasn't the type to encourage sympathy. She straightened her back and shoved the test into her satchel.

"I've just lost valedictorian. And with that, I lost the scholarship to Vanderbilt University," Bettie's voice cracked. "Serves me right. I can't be that smart if I make choices this dumb." She turned and walked down the hall towards the exit.

Joe watched her hips sway under her navy-blue skirt. Athena, Joe, and I sighed together.

3

Aphrodite Enters

The sobbing. The sobbing. The sobbing. I have to admit I quickly grow tired of human dramatics—not on the stage because I love a good show—but in the small sphere of their own minds.

Bettie ranted at herself. "Why am I such an idiot? Nora even warned me! Who cares about that stupid old play? Now, I'll never get out of Nashville. I'll never escape this place. That scholarship was my golden ticket. Now, I'll end up marrying a local guy, like Bubba, and popping out a baby every year, just like Momma. I'll end up like her, worn out and angry. She was pretty too, when she was young. I'll be fat and ugly, listening to my husband talk about football and country music. I wanted more from life." Her crying had produced hiccups, and I took their distraction as an opportunity to enter her mind and end her pity party.

You'll still be salutatorian and earn a scholarship to Peabody College Teaching School. She could hear me now because I had become that voice in Bettie's head that offered an alternative perspective. The voice that tries to stop you from drowning in the primitive world of your emotions. You know the one. It makes you decide to sit up, wash your face, and get on with life. Mortals should be happy when that voice appears.

"A teacher. Who wants to be a teacher? Yellow-toothed from drinking coffee all day and jealous of your students, like Mrs. Stark," she argued.

Mrs. Stark was jealous of you so that must mean there is something worth envying.

"Women are always jealous of me—even when I don't do anything. It isn't my fault her stupid old husband flirted with me." Bettie answered. "Women always hate me."

Better get used to it.

Even as a goddess, I have unfairly been blamed and accused of actions that I played no part in. I shared my knowledge with Bettie.

A beautiful, vivacious woman frightens other women. They know they can't compete and so they become petty and catty. The gossip and assumptions won't ever stop, so you had better find a way to turn your magnetism into power instead of rejecting your gifts.

"Even Momma rejected me—made me move out of my own home because her creepy boyfriend paid too much attention to me." Bettie sat up on the bed and punched the pillow. "Thank goodness Daddy's new wife took me in and is nice."

Even when we enter a mortal, they still have their free will. We can't make them do anything they don't want to do. I thought Bettie was going to get up. Unfortunately, she decided to continue crying.

"I'll never get out of this town." She buried her face in her pillow and started another round of sobbing. Humans say crying is cathartic. I say it is self-indulgent.

Hoping to find an angle I could use to cheer her up, I asked her to think about what she had lost. I suspected the goal of winning the scholarship was driven by her ego, which was determined to be little Miss Perfect, and not what her authentic self really wanted.

How would the Vanderbilt scholarship change your life?

"I was going to major in English literature. I love to read and that would let me study all the classics and dig deep into them."

My heart sunk at her answer. I realized that Athena probably would have been a better fit for her, but it was too late now. We aren't allowed to pop into a mortal, try their life on for size, and then pop out if it isn't a perfect fit. I would need another turning point, created by Bettie's actions, before I could leave. I probed deeper.

What would you have done with that English degree? Teach?

"I was going to marry someone smart and sophisticated—probably a professor. I would have had a salon, just like a French woman. All my friends would be intellectuals. We would have tea and discuss Tolstoy and Faulkner. My husband and I would live in New York and spend every summer traveling."

I was appalled at her answer. Both Athena and I had seen something special in Bettie. Now, it sounded like she didn't see something special in herself.

Don't tell me you wanted to go to college to earn your MRS degree? You have so much potential. Men are fun, but don't lose yourself in a supporting role. You can be the star of your own life. You can still travel. Get that teaching degree and move to New York.

Bettie shook her head. It was clear that a job in teaching could not be used as a carrot. If her heart was set on marriage, I at least wanted to make sure she knew she could have a higher standard than Bubba, and she didn't need Vanderbilt University to get it.

Europe is at war again, and it is just a matter of time before your country gets involved. Once you have a degree it opens doors to new jobs. Go work for Oak Ridge, there are plenty of smart engineers over there.

"What's Oak Ridge?" Bettie wondered.

Rats. Sometimes I start riffing inside my mortal's head and forget that they don't have omniscient knowledge like me. Zeus hates it when we reveal secrets. "That's the job of the Oracle at Delphi," he reminds us. Hopefully he wasn't paying attention to me. I changed the subject.

Let's not think about the future right now. We have to make sure you make your sacrifice worth it. You will be the best Lady Macbeth that Hume-Fogg High has ever seen. Even Mrs. Stark will have to admit that you have talent and feel bad that she was so mean to you.

Encouraged, Bettie sat up. I knew that, with mortals, taking physical action can improve their mindset.

Now go wash your face and brush your hair.

Bettie got off the bed and went into the bathroom. As she looked in the mirror, I couldn't help but feel the thrill of being inside this mortal body. I had chosen wisely––thick raven black hair, dazzling blue eyes, flawless skin, buoyant breasts, and a radiant smile. What a body to experience a mortal existence in!

Epictetus, the Greek philosopher, described the human condition as, "A little wisp of soul carrying a corpse." I disagree. The human body is an endless source of sensory and physical excitement.

There is a certain boredom found in the physical perfection and powers of an immortal. We have no sense of time or urgency. To be in a human body, to realize that it is continually racing towards decay and death, is exciting. Each sight, smell, sound, taste, and touch is something to savor. Even the wild confusion of emotions tie into the body with racing heartbeats, breathlessness, and dilated eyes. Bettie's human body was a magnificent vehicle, and I was going to enjoy my ride as copilot.

Still looking in the mirror, Bettie gave herself a pep talk. "It doesn't matter that Barton Murphey will get valedictorian. I'll still get salutatorian and get to give the commencement speech."

And that speech will be the best Hume-Fogg High School has ever heard.

#

The final semester of senior year wound to a close, and Bettie was indeed a magnificent Lady Macbeth. Mr. Stark made a point of telling her after the show, but Bettie wisely turned her back without acknowledging him.

One day, Bettie was walking home from school alone when a red roadster pulled up beside her. A hunk in his early twenties called, "Hey beautiful! Are there any more at home like you?"

Hmmm, he's so handsome. Look at that strong chin and broad shoulders.

"And he's driving a car which means he has money. Even my dad still has to take the bus, but I'm going to play it cool," Bettie thought.

Bettie glanced over her shoulder and kept walking, but she knew his eyes were on her butt, so she swung her hips sensuously. "Why are you worrying about what's at home?" She flirted as he drove slowly alongside her. She glanced coyly, but stopped and gave him a huge smile, as she recognized him. "Why you're Billy Neal."

"That's right. I went to East High." She walked closer to the convertible and leaned forward noticing the twinkle in his green eyes and his thick brown hair. He looked like a teen idol and wore his high school letterman jacket over a white-collared shirt.

Billy preened. "Back in my glory days—you ever see me play?" His car purred in idle, and Bettie felt like a motor was purring inside her. She couldn't imagine that Billy Neal, star football and basketball player, was paying attention to her.

"I watched you trounce us every time. I was a reporter for *The Fogg-Horn* and it was no fun to write about our defeat." Bettie stood up so that she could display her breasts better, and shifted her books to one hip. "So, what are your doing now that you've graduated?"

"Right now, I'm asking you on a date," Billy said with a cocky grin.

"Me?" Bettie squealed and then remembered to play it cool.

"Well, you're lucky. My Momma never let me date, but I happen to be living with my Dad now. He doesn't care what I do."

"Your folks are divorced?" She saw disapproval flicker across his face.

"Uh-huh." Bettie studied his car while she searched for the words. She looked up and met his eyes, "My Dad had some troubles, but he's changed now, so things are better for both of them," said Bettie, although she didn't really believe things were better off for her Momma.

"You like to dance?" Billy asked and whistled "In the Mood" by Glenn Miller.

Bettie swooned. She'd always loved a boy who could whistle. "I don't know how, but I'm a quick study."

"I bet you'll turn out to be a real jive bomber. Let me get your number and I'll call ya tonight." Billy said. Bettie pulled a paper out of her notebook, wrote down her number with a little heart at the end, and handed it to him. She shivered as he purposely touched her fingers as he took it. "I'll give you a ring," he said with a wink. Bettie hummed with delight as Billy revved his engine and zipped away.

True to his word, Billy called that night and asked her out for Saturday. He picked her up in his hot little convertible and drove over to Jefferson Street, where all the coolest clubs were located.

Bettie wore her one nice dress. It was Kelly green and a hand-me-down from her mother. Bettie had hemmed it to the knee and nipped it in to show off her waist. Nora had loaned her a pearl neck-lace. Ready to dance, she wore bobby sox and black loafers on her feet.

Bettie looked at the marquee as they got out. "Artie Shaw. My goodness, I've never seen anything other than the high school jazz band."

Billy took her by the hand. "When I heard his tour was coming down here, I knew I had to see him. You are in for a treat. His music washes over you and gets you right here," he said, putting his fist against his sternum. "It's like something in the beat just makes you want to dance." He paid the entrance fee and guided her into the club.

The large dance hall had a band at one end and tables around the sides of the room. The floor was crowded. Dancers spun and kicked. Some of the boys flipped the girls and others slid between their legs. The room was spinning with excitement.

"I'm not sure I can do this," said Bettie.

"Come'on doll," said Billy taking her out onto the floor. "The steps are pretty simple and then you just add layers on it when you get better. Triple step to the left, triple step to the right, now rock step." Billy demonstrated slowly.

"Like this?" Bettie tried to copy Billy, but she was stiff and flat-footed. She was trying so hard to be the perfect student. I could feel her joy disappear as she struggled to learn. I love to dance and couldn't wait to feel the swing. I gave her some tips.

You will do fine. Just get out of your head and into your body. Feel the beat and you will intuitively know how to follow it. Get up on your toes and don't be so stompy. If you keep moving, it doesn't matter if you get off beat; you can get right back on it. This isn't a test. Don't over think it.

She took my advice, and with Billy's patient tutoring, was able to master the basic steps. It didn't take long for her to add some spins and kicks. Billy was a terrific lead, and once Bettie got out of her head, she was able to follow. They danced for an hour straight and then Billy suggested they take a break and get a Coke.

"This is so much fun," said Bettie, still panting a little from the dancing.

"I knew you'd be a natural," he said and stole a kiss. Warmth flooded though Bettie and she leaned into him. "What do you say we go for a drive?"

Play hard to get. His kisses are wonderful, but so is his dancing. Let's make this evening last. You need to train a man how to treat you from the very first date. Build the anticipation.

Bettie put her hand on his strong bicep and gave a little squeeze. "Let's dance awhile longer," Bettie said. "You are a terrific teacher."

The pair danced another two hours before Bettie agreed to go for a drive. Billy drove down to the river and parked in a spot hidden by overhanging willow trees. He turned towards her and caressed her face. "Your skin is so soft." He traced a line under her nose. "I loved how you got a little sweat mustache when we were dancing."

"I did not," said Bettie, embarrassed. She rubbed her hand on her face.

"Oh right, ladies don't perspire. Well, I loved the way you glowed––right here." He kissed below her nose with tiny little pecks then dropped to her lips and slowly transitioned from pecks to French kissing.

I swooned. This man knew how to kiss.

Bettie followed her instincts and kissed him back. He made a low growl of pleasure. One of Billy's hands threaded through her hair and the other cupped her jaw. His hands, his kisses, and his whispers flooded her with relaxation. She surrendered to the sensations and kissed him passionately, her hands squeezing his manly shoulders and strong back. Billy's hand caressed her ankle and slowly moved up her leg. She knew she should tell him to stop, but it felt so good. His fingers climbed the back of her thigh and started to slide under her panties. She stiffened.

"I think you had better take me home," she said.

"Aw, come on." He held his hands up in surrender. "I won't push you. I'll keep my hands on top of fabric at all times—fair?"

"I think I'm giving you the wrong impression. I don't want to lead you on."

"I know you're a good girl, but you're so gorgeous. You can't blame me for trying," he smiled a goofy smile and took her hand in his. "I'll behave, I promise." He leaned forward and kissed her ear and then slid along her cheek, "Just keep giving me your magic kisses."

Bettie sighed with desire and started to weaken. I was getting lost in the sensations of Billy's hands and kisses, but that good girl in Bettie wouldn't shut up. She gently pushed Billy away and scooted out of his embrace, towards the car door.

"I really need you to take me home now."

Billy sighed and started the engine. He was frustrated, but I knew he'd be calling Bettie again.

#

Graduation approached, and I helped Bettie craft her commencement address which we optimistically called "Class of 1940––Looking Forward." Bettie practiced her speech nightly in front of the mirror. She grew increasingly worried about what she would wear because the girls had to wear a white evening gown for graduation. Any time she brought up the topic with her dad, he ranted that he wasn't made of money.

Go kiss up to Lulu, I suggested. She's a woman, and she'll understand. You know if she asks your dad to buy you a dress, he won't say no.

"He never says no to her," Bettie agreed. "She's got him wrapped around her little finger."

Pay attention and take lessons. That's a good skill for a girl to have in this world.

After much pleading from Bettie and Lulu, her father finally agreed, but stubbornly waited until the day of graduation to take Bettie shopping.

They entered Morris Department Store, and Bettie raced ahead to the evening-wear department. It didn't take long before she found the perfect dress. It was white with thin straps on the bodice. The best part was the tulle skirt that flared as she twirled in front of the mirror.

"Can I have this one?" She asked her dad.

"You look like an angel—so grown up." Bettie was surprised to hear the emotion cracking her dad's voice. She glanced at him, but he busied himself with lighting a cigarette. "How much does it cost?"

Bettie showed him the tag and held her breath.

"Nope. Too much." He stood up and walked to the bargain rack. "How about this one?" He held up a conservative white dress.

"That looks like a sack. I could sew a dress prettier than that."

"Well then why didn't you? Why did you have to buy a dress and waste my money?" There was so much anger in his tone that Bettie knew better than to continue to argue.

"It's fine. Let me try it on." She went into the dressing room and took off the magical tulle dress and slipped on the cotton one. It had long sleeves with puffs at the shoulders and a high neckline.

Bettie looked at herself and started to cry. "It's this or nothing. Why can't he let me have something special for once in my life?"

His reaction was strange. Maybe he doesn't like it that you've turned into such an attractive woman. Just get the dress. We can find some jewelry to make it look better.

Her dad purchased the dress while Bettie and I visited the jewelry displays. After all, the dress is important, but never underestimate the power of accessories.

I am a perfect example. When I first appeared on Mt. Olympus, all the male gods wanted me. Almost immediately, Poseidon and Ares began performing dangerous stunts to gain my attention. The female goddesses were green with jealousy, and Zeus knew my presence would be the cause of endless turmoil. He decided to marry me off immediately and chose Hephaestus as my husband.

The son of Hera and Zeus, Hephaestus had been borne small and ugly with a red, bawling face. In disgust, Hera threw him off of Mt. Olympus. He landed in the ocean and the force broke his leg and made him crippled. In the depths of the ocean, he was taken in by the sea-nymph Thetis, and she raised him as her son in her under-water grotto. The nymphs taught him metalworking and he became the god of volcanoes, fire, and the forge. Eventually, he was admitted back to Mt. Olympus after trapping Hera in a golden throne he crafted, then earning her apology.

I was furious for having to marry an ugly, crippled God when Olympus was full of perfect, handsome alternatives. On our wedding night, I refused to yield my virginity to Hephaestus. He left the bed and went down into his forging shop. He came back and presented me with the wedding gift he had just crafted.

It was a girdle, a wide belt, made of gold. On the surface, he had filigreed images of doves, roses, and seashells. The images were connected with spiraling vines and accented with precious stones such as sapphires and emeralds, plus my favorites––pearl, coral and abalone shell. I fell in love with it immediately and, it turned out, the belt gave me the power to make any man fall in love with me. I gleefully accepted the belt and allowed Hephaestus to consummate our marriage. Accessories can bring great satisfaction and joy.

#

Bettie didn't dare ask for accessories or anything else. She brooded about how unfair her father treated her.

While on the bus on her way home, Bettie searched for the bag so she could take another look at the dress.

"Where is it?" She asked her dad, panic tightening her throat.

"What?" He asked.

"The bag? My dress! Don't you have it?"

"I thought you had it," said her dad, sharing her panic.

They jumped off the bus at the next stop but, by the time they returned to the store, it had closed. Bettie cupped her hands and peered in the window. "There it is, the bag is still on the counter."

Her dad shook his head and patted her on the shoulder. "Sorry, Honey."

"What am I going to do?" Bettie wailed. "I can't wear my ratty school clothes. I have to have an evening gown."

Her dad shrugged. He'd never understood the drama over the dress in the first place and had only agreed to please his wife. "Well, let's go home. We've got to get cleaned up before your graduation tonight." The bus stopped, and he got on.

"No," shouted Bettie.

"Suit yourself," he said as the bus doors closed, leaving Bettie on the curb.

I took this moment to intervene. I wasn't going to let our big speech be ruined, and I knew she needed to look beautiful to do her best. I suggested a solution.

There are a bunch of young women staying at the YWCA. Maybe you should ask to borrow a dress.

Bettie ran across the street and into the Y. Boldly, she knocked on every door, pleading for a dress. Soon the hall was filled with women expressing their concern. That is the strangest thing about women. We can be so catty and awful towards each other, but, at other times, we bond together like an Olympic team. Any woman who has been crying-drunk in a public restroom has experienced the camaraderie of her sisters in a moment of crisis.

Finally, a hero emerged.

"Will this do?" The pretty blonde asked holding out a white organdy dress. "We look like we are about the same size." Another girl volunteered to let Bettie use her room to change, and the entire hall cheered as she came out and modeled the dress, which fit her perfectly.

"It's like the fairy godmother scene in Cinderella," joked a girl.

Exactly.

4

College Days

After graduation, Bettie continued to live with her father and Lulu while attending Peabody College. She worked hard in her education classes, but her true interest, as it had been in high school, was theater. She joined the Peabody Players and kept busy performing in seven plays, including a Community Theater production. The all-girls teacher prep school was a tad boring for me. I was much more interested in the opposite sex, but Bettie loved the environment free of distractions and petty jealousies over boys.

Lucky for me, she continued dating the handsome Billy. He was just my type, a strong alpha male like Ares, the God of War, Battle Lust, and Manliness. For those of you that have never dated an alpha, their appeal might seem odd. After all, neither Hera nor Zeus loved their first borne son once he revealed his anger and love of conflict.

Ah, but I loved Ares. He was so virile and handsome. I adored his warrior posture and fit, muscular body. He could run for miles with thighs and calves that felt like iron. The fires of passion burned in his eyes, and his full lips were made for kissing. I loved the way it felt to be held in his strong arms, his hands caressing my body with a feeling of ownership. When an alpha holds you in his possessive grip, it makes you feel beautiful like a prize. The biggest thrill of an alpha is their supreme confidence. You can't help but feel safe and protected when you are with them. Of course, once the mist of lust has faded, those same qualities might not seem as attractive. However, it is a fun ride while it lasts. Although not inhabited by Ares, Billy was a true alpha male, and Bettie was nearly as smitten as me.

Billy was a hometown sports hero and, even though he was out of high school, he was still recognized and chatted up all around town. He seemed like one of those young men whose glory would never fade.

Billy's father owned a car dealership. New Deal programs and defense industry development in Tennessee had revived the economy and his business prospered. To help with publicity at the dealership, he encouraged Billy to take out different cars and drive them around town. Bettie felt like a celebrity on Billy's arm and in the latest cars. It was a dramatic improvement from the poverty-filled years of her recent past.

In Billy's arms, she discovered her sexuality. Although she never let him go all the way, they spent many hours in the back of Billy's car in extended foreplay. Bettie would lose herself in the feel of his kisses and his hands exploring every inch of her body. Billy relentlessly pressed her to go farther, but she always refused.

I have to admit that I was surprised at what a good girl she was. She had internalized the warnings of her mother about men and was terrified of earning the label of "share crop," the slang for a slutty girl. Whatever the word, I detest the concept of *slut*. Women use it as much as men as a socially acceptable way attacking their competition and sublimating their sexual jealousy. An Aphrodite woman always runs the risk of earning that label, and the fear of earning it is how other people control us.

Betty instinctively knew that. Because she was poor, it was even more important for her to have a sterling reputation. A rich girl might be able to have sex with a steady boyfriend, but a poor girl would instantly be called "trashy." She had dreams and aspirations. She was not only terrified of an unplanned pregnancy, but also of the social isolation a "share crop" label would rain down upon her.

However, she had a high sex drive, loved the heavy petting, and did everything but "it."

One evening, while the lovebirds were making out in his car, the music on the radio station stopped for an important announcement. "From the NBC newsroom in New York, President Roosevelt said in a statement that the Japanese have attacked Pearl Harbor in Hawaii, from the air."

Bettie and Billy looked at each other in shock. They untangled their bodies and straightened their clothes.

"I've got to get home," said Billy and started the car.

"Are you going to join up?" Bettie asked.

"I already had to register for the Selective Service. I guess, if they need me, they'll call up my number in the draft." Billy fiddled with the radio station, but each one was filled with commentary about the attack. He turned it off, and they drove on silence.

I sighed to myself. Like Ares, Billy was a coward. When storm monster Typhon attacked Mt. Olympus, Ares was the first run away. He fled to Egypt and turned himself into a fish. During the Trojan War, Ares flew into battle, and the mortal Diomedes speared him in his gut. Ares howled so loudly, it sounded like 10,000 men. He raced to Mt. Olympus and cried to Zeus, who shamed him for is weakness.

After Pearl Harbor, a true warrior would have immediately joined, wanting to avenge the attack on his homeland. Instead, Billy was going to wait and see if his number got called. I hate war, but I hate cowardice too. I didn't need to point this out to Bettie, it didn't take her long to recognize the fact herself.

All of her brothers enlisted immediately. Her older brother, William, became an engineer for the Army Corps of Engineers and was sent off to build bridges in Europe. Jimmie was a gunner's mate on a destroyer, and Jack was a cook on a destroyer escort. Every week Bettie would write V-mail letters to her siblings, mail them on Saturday, and go on a date with Billy that night.

The movies would always start with a newsreel about the war and then follow it with a propaganda cartoon. Bettie wondered if Billy felt as awkward as she did, sitting in a theater filled with women and old men.

#

"Come on, Bettie," Billy pleaded during a frustrating make-out session in his car.

Bettie pushed him away, straightened her skirt, and reclipped her bra. "I told you, Billy, I don't want to get pregnant. Look at my mom—six kids to raise by herself. I thought you respected me?" She gave him an accusing glare.

"I do, Baby, but we've been together for a couple of years." He looked at Bettie to see if he was swaying her. She had her arms and legs crossed with a touch-me-not look on her face. Her body felt rigid and tight like it always did when she shut off her sex drive. I sighed with frustration. That girl had made virginity into a monument that testified to her goodness.

Billy sighed too and buttoned up his shirt. "Look, I've been thinking..."

The seriousness of his tone sent prickles of alarm through Bettie and she turned to face him. "About what?"

"They called my draft number. I've got to report to basic training in two weeks."

Bettie patted Billy's thigh and nodded her support. The silence stretched between them.

Billy cleared his throat and took Bettie's hand in his. "So, I've been thinking. Let's get married."

Bettie stared into his hopeful face in shock. "Married? But I'm not even done with college. I'm only a junior." Bettie forced herself not to yank her hand from Billy's. In her head, she saw a steel bear trap of marriage, open and waiting to be triggered.

"Come on Baby, what if I get killed in the war? Don't you want to grant me my dying wish?"

"Don't talk like that." Bettie felt panic waterfall down her back.

Tell him you don't want to start a family. You need to finish your degree.

"I'm not ready for a baby. You know how important getting an education is to me." Bettie had to use all her will power to not jump out of the car. She leaned towards the door and tapped her finger on the handle.

"Look, I'll be careful not to get you pregnant, and you can keep going to school. Don't you love me?"

"I do love you Billy, but I have dreams."

"What dreams?" He did not hide his frustration. "You don't think you are going to make it as an actress, do you? All those plays you're always in?" Bettie shook her head no. "Well, you can be a teacher, until we have kids. I don't have a problem with that." Billy pulled her rigid body towards him. "Come on, Baby. I love you. Don't you owe me this?"

He kissed her and caressed her face. He nibbled her cheek towards her ear and whispered, "I'm scared I'm not going to come back."

Bettie felt a rush of sympathy. She thought, "Maybe I should grant him his wish."

Are you crazy! Don't marry him. You're only 20 years old. You have your entire life ahead of you.

"Well, he's scared," she argued with me silently.

So, what if he's scared? Everyone is. Be sympathetic and supportive. Write him letters. You don't have to marry him. What if he gets killed?

"Then there would be a widow's pension." She shook the mercenary thought out of her head.

Even I think that's a horrible thought. Listen to me. Do not marry him. Have sex with him before he ships out, but you don't have to get married.

"Never," Bettie said and I could feel her repressing me. "I'm not that kind of girl. I have to be a virgin on my wedding night."

Billy interrupted our exchange with a slow sweet kiss and those magic hands. "Come on Baby, don't you love me? Every girl wants to marry their first love—right? Why wait a few years when you know we'll end up together anyways?"

Don't do it!

Bettie would no longer listen to me. She sighed and gave Billy a half smile. "Okay. I mean, yes. Yes, I will become your wife."

Billy hooted with relief and hugged her tight. Looking into his dilated eyes as he grinned into Bettie's, my heart dropped. I saw lust in his eyes and knew that's why he wanted to get married—to get laid. If only Bettie had not been so virtuous, she could have avoided this dilemma. Billy didn't realize that he'd have plenty of opportunities once he went overseas, but I did. Ares loved the sexual spoils of war.

Bettie went home and didn't tell a soul. On Saturday morning, February 18, 1943, she put on her black jersey dress and rode the bus to Gallatin, a small town 30 miles from Nashville. Bettie and Billy married in the courthouse with two strangers as witnesses.

On the bus ride home, they sat in silence holding hands. "What have I done?" Bettie asked herself.

In her mind, we both heard the bear trap slamming shut.

#

The newlyweds returned to Billy's parents' house. Billy's parents graciously left home for the evening to give them privacy and allowed them to use their master bedroom with its double bed.

Bettie fluffed her hair in the bathroom, put on red lipstick, then blotted it off. She wore her best ivory slip which fell to her knees. She rubbed her cold hands together and stared into the mirror. I think she was waiting for one of my pep talks.

Tonight's the night you get to give in to all those urges. It's like dancing, remember, don't get into your head, just stay in your body.

"Are you ever coming out of there?" Billy called. He lay naked in the bed. He breathed into his cupped hand to check his breath and rubbed them together in anticipation.

Bettie opened the door and stepped into the room. Billy whistled. Bettie tentatively approached the bed when he patted it. She sat on the edge.

Billy ran his hand from her down her spine and squeezed her hip. "You look gorgeous, Baby." He caressed her back a moment more. "Come on, Baby, lay here beside me. Just relax. You're going to love this."

I laughed to myself. When had a virgin ever enjoyed her deflowering? *Awkward* and *painful* tend to be the words most often used to describe it.

Bettie lay next to Billy, and he leaned over her, kissing her nervousness away. His hands slid down the silky fabric until he found the hem, then he started to pull it off. Betty stiffened.

Tell him to slow down. It won't hurt as much if he takes his time.

"I can't tell him what to do. That's embarrassing," Bettie argued with me.

Billy removed her slip.

"Let me just look at you," he whispered. "What a body. You're every man's dream, curves and silky skin." He gave her an endless kiss, one leading into the next. One deep, the other shallow, and sensual with silky lips sliding over each other. "You know that?"

Bettie felt dazed from arousal and shook her head to come back to earth. "Know what?"

"How beautiful you are...how perfect...how desirable," as he spoke Billy positioned himself on top of her. "Just relax. It's only going to hurt a minute." He entered her, and she tightened at the pain. Instead of slowing down, Billy plowed ahead and then got caught up in his own sensations. It was a quick trip to the final thrust with a pull out onto her tummy.

Breathing heavily, Billy lay back. Bettie lay unmoving, surprised and a little disappointed. This is what everyone made such a big deal about? Dancing with Billy was a thousand times sexier and fun. She sighed.

Billy wiped his spunk off her with an old sock. "How does it feel to be a woman?" He asked, his voice filled with pride. He pulled her in for a deep kiss. Betty wondered how soon she would be expected to do it again.

"Hmmm. I'm kind of sore." She started to get out of the bed. "We'd better get dressed. Your parents will be back from dinner soon, and we need to change the sheets for them."

Billy closed his eyes. "Sure, just let me take a little nap first." She felt agitated and restless, but Billy fell into a comfortable slumber.

Bettie shrugged and went to take a shower. She smiled realizing it could be a long hot one without anyone knocking on the door, telling her to hurry up and stop wasting water.

#

Billy went to boot camp in Mississippi, and Bettie continued living with his folks. They had a quiet household and, although there didn't seem to be any passion in their marriage, his parents were respectful and polite towards each other. Bettie envied how much nicer Billy's childhood must have been compared to her home filled with children and arguing. She continued going to Peabody College and worked as a secretary in the evenings.

The war effort was in full swing. Bettie rolled bandages with her sister, Goldie, at the Red Cross. The Neals had turned their front and back yards into Victory Gardens to help extend their food choices beyond what was available through rationing.

One humid summer day, Bettie was on her hands and knees weeding. She had her shoulder-length hair tied back in a ponytail.

"You're such a hard worker. Those weeds don't stand a chance against you," said Mrs. Neal as she roughed up the soil with a hoe to improve drainage.

Bettie shoed away a fly with her gloved hand and kept weeding. "This is nothing. When I was in grade school, my Daddy bought a farm."

"Oh, I didn't realize your people were rural." Mrs. Neal had abandoned her hoeing and stood in the shade, blotting her perspiration with an embroidered hanky.

Bettie kept looking down and rolled her eyes at the false sincerity. She knew perfectly well that the Neals considered the Pages to be white trash. Her parents' divorce was bad enough, but Momma worked as a hairdresser in the poor part of town. It was not a place Mrs. Neal would frequent, but also not so far away that she wouldn't be privy to gossip about her Momma's philandering boyfriend and the antics of the wild Page kids.

"It was 48 acres, off of the Memphis Highway." She thought back to those lean years on the farm, searching for a happy memory. "We had some chickens. Us kids would get a couple of feathers and blow on them. We would duel each other to see who could keep them in the air the longest. We called it Fighting Feathers." Bettie chuckled to herself.

"What crops did your father raise?" Mrs. Neal asked. She drank water, and Bettie noticed she didn't offer to get any for her.

"Not much, mostly sweet potatoes. The land was rocky and hard to plant in. We had to haul water up a hill from the nearest spring. My brothers, William and Jimmie, and me had to do most of the work, since we were the oldest, and Momma had her hands full with three little ones." She glanced up at Mrs. Neal, surprised to see she had her full attention. "My Daddy promised to pay us five cents for each bucket of rocks we removed, and five cents for each bucket of water we hauled. Jimmie and I worked hard and kept track of what we earned in a little notebook."

"How much money did you earn?" Mrs. Neal's tone was skeptical. She obviously had her own opinions about Bettie's daddy.

"We earned $300 each." Bettie scooped up the pile of weeds and dumped them in the aluminum trash can. She cracked her back and knelt down to weed the next row.

"Did he pay up?"

"No. We kept waiting. Finally, after about a year, we brought him our little book, showed him our figures, and politely asked him for our wages. He laughed and laughed. 'You didn't really think I was going to give you any money for your work—did you? We don't have a pot to piss in and you want $300 EACH?' He just kept laughing. Jimmie and I stomped out of the room." Bettie shook her head. "I was only nine, and Jimmie was eight. What a mean trick to play on little kids."

"Once you knew he wasn't going to pay you, how did he get you to work?" Bettie wasn't used to Mrs. Neal showing so much interest in her. Most of their time, she sat quietly knitting and allowing her husband to do all the talking.

"Well..." Bettie didn't want to reveal the next part of the story, on the off-chance Mrs. Neal hadn't heard it through the grapevine. She ran through the memory in her mind.

One night, while they were eating dinner, they had heard a pounding on the door.

"Open up you bastard. I'm going to kill you." Bettie, Momma and the kids stared at each other in confusion, but Daddy had jumped up and hopped out of a window in the back. Shaking, her Momma had slowly opened the door and been confronted with their neighbor, holding a shotgun in one hand, and squeezing the arm of his crying 15 year old daughter in the other.

"Where is he?" The neighbor demanded. When Momma told him that her husband was gone, he had cussed a blue-streak. "Your no-good husband knocked up my Rosie." He shoved his daughter into the room. "Pregnant! What with you having six kids and us having a house full of our own, who's gonna to take care of this brat?"

The color drained from Momma's face. Bettie was terrified that Rosie was going to have to live with them, and she'd have even more diapers to change and wash. But Momma had finally had enough.

"You can ask him about that. I'm getting a divorce and moving off this God-forsaken farm."

The version Bettie told Mrs. Neal was limited to, "My mom had had enough of farm life. They got a divorce, and we moved to Nashville with her.

#

Bettie's last semester in college was devoted to student teaching English at the demonstration high school. For her first day of teaching, Bettie wore a long-sleeved shirt, buttoned to the top, with a blue A-line skirt. She entered the classroom with her mentor, Mrs. Smith, a seasoned teacher with twenty years of experience.

"Now class," said Mrs. Smith, "this is Mrs. Neal, your new teacher." A wolf whistle sounded from the back of the class. Bettie stiffened. "Now boys, be respectful. Mrs. Neal will finish teaching our Hamlet unit." With a brisk nod, her mentor left the room.

Bettie set her book bag down and wiped her hands on her skirt. "Okay class, Mrs. Smith said you were on page 24."

"I'd like to see Mrs. Neal kneeling," whispered a football player to his buddy next to him. Bettie heard and cleared her throat.

"So, would anyone like to start reading?" Silence greeted her. "Okay, I'll start. I'm on Act 1 Scene 1. 'O, that this too, too solid flesh would melt/Thaw and resolve itself into a dew.'" Bettie heard snickers. Even to her ears, Hamlet contemplating suicide had suddenly turned into something that sounded erotic.

She glanced up at the sea of 17 year old faces. She was only 21 and felt like a lamb among wolves. Bettie gestured to a girl in the front row. "What is your name?"

"Mary," the girl said and several kids snickered.

Bettie wondered what they were laughing at. She smoothed her hair. "Mary, please read for us."

The girl shrugged. "I don't feel like it." Her defiance rattled Bettie. She had never heard a girl be so disrespectful. More laughter erupted and she heard a student start drumming under the table top.

Taking a deep breath, Bettie tried to regroup. She turned to write on the board and heard another whistle. Fighting back tears, she sat down at the teacher desk, desperate to hide and have some protection from these monsters. She scanned the room for a sympathetic face and found only sneers or predatory gleams. "Read silently to yourselves." Her voice cracked. "Finish the next three scenes by tomorrow for a pop quiz."

A collective groan greeted those words. Bettie made her face as stern as she could and gestured for the class to read. She picked up her copy and hid behind it while the class ignored her and talked to each other. Several kids started walking around the room and two boys in the back played keep-away with a girl's pencil pouch. Huddled behind the teacher desk, Bettie pretended not to notice.

#

The semester passed at a snail's pace and left Bettie with one discovery. "I will never teach again," she shouted to Billy as she spoke to him over the phone. He had been transferred to San Francisco to await deployment. She heard his laughter and longed to feel his strong arms around her. "Graduation is on Friday and then I'm free. I can't wait to see you again."

"You buy your bus ticket already?" He asked.

"I bought it the day you sent the money. My sister Goldie is coming with me, so you don't need to worry about the trip."

"You and Goldie together? The Page tomatoes?" He laughed. "I think I have twice as much to worry about. You two will have a line of men following you all the way from Tennessee to California." Bettie was relieved to hear the joking in his tone. Sometimes, Billy could be so pessimistic, but today he seemed to be in good spirits.

"I can't wait to see you, Tiger. I've got some extra sweet kisses saved up for you," Bettie purred.

"Can't wait to kiss you, feel you, hold you. I've already got two days leave for when you arrive." Bettie made her little kitten mew and Billy answered it with his tiger growl. "See you soon, Baby," he whispered and the call ended.

5

San Francisco

Bettie had a passionate reunion with Billy. It was sweetened by their separation, and the knowledge that he would soon be fighting in the Pacific Theater. On their last evening, Billy blew most of his savings for a night on the town. He took her to the Cliff House, located on a bluff above the beach. It was the fanciest restaurant Bettie had ever seen, much less patronized.

Billy, in typical Ares fashion, ordered the meal. It seemed like an homage to me. It began with shrimp cocktails and oysters, and continued through with abalone steaks, sourdough bread, salad and chilled white wine. Bettie had never had seafood, but she gamely tried it all and loved it. She never drank alcohol and asked the waiter to bring her milk instead.

Billy teased her and called her a hick. She toasted him with an oyster shell. "Here's to two hicks in the Big City!"

"Welcome to California, Baby. They call it the New America, and I think you are going to like it."

Bettie nodded and gestured towards the ocean. I looked at the ocean, and then at all the handsome men filling the restaurant.

Oh, yes. We are going to love it here.

#

After Billy shipped out, Goldie and Bettie quickly settled into California life. They shared a studio apartment. Goldie got a job on the factory floor of Enterprise Engine and Foundry Company. Bettie, who had won a blue ribbon in high school as the fastest typist, secured a job as a secretary for the sales manager.

"Goldie, the Riveter," as Bettie called her, had to wear shapeless overalls to work. The rules for females were strict——no hair could emerge from the bandana, and nail polish, lipstick and make-up were forbidden.

In the front office, Bettie was encouraged to look feminine and wore sweaters, knee-length skirts, and make-up. She bought nylons when possible, but, once they were rationed, she had Goldie draw a line down the back of her leg. Playfully jealous, Goldie called her "Betty Grable."

On the weekends, Goldie made up for her work-day austerity. Not used to having money, she spent her wages on clothes. Fashion had a military tone, with padded shoulders, single-button jackets, A-line skirts, high pompadours, and lots of lipstick. Goldie spent her check as soon as she received it.

Bettie was more cautious. She always saved at least 10% of her paycheck. She had a suitcase under the bed that she would put cash into after payday. It made her feel secure to sleep on top of that money and know she could be independent.

Her one indulgence was accessories. She bought basic dresses and skirts, but made them look like different outfits with belts, collars, and jewelry. She and Goldie pooled their fashion resources so that they had gloves, hats, purses and shoes to match every outfit.

"A coordinated woman is a confident woman," Goldie said, parroting the women's magazines.

Goldie, always a social butterfly, soon made a group of friends. Bettie, Goldie, and the girls joined the USO Hospitality House at Civic Center. Young women were encouraged to volunteer their time to hang out at Hospitality House and chat with the soldiers, play Ping-Pong and party games. The USO would organize chaperoned events and dances.

In the beginning, Bettie would tell the soldiers that she was married. She didn't want to get their hopes up, and she wanted to be true to Billy. Except, Goldie and her friends were all single, and Bettie started to feel like a matronly chaperone.

I couldn't hide my annoyance. Bettie was acting like Penelope, faithfully weaving and turning away suitors, while, at the same time, Odysseus was sleeping with Circe and Calypso. The double standard of marriage incenses me.

Why not take your ring off? Billy doesn't need to know. Goldie won't tell.

I suggested to her one night while she sat alone. Her friends were all dancing, and she had turned down one handsome hunk after another with her marital status.

"I don't know. He's over there fighting, so I should stay loyal."

Didn't it feel like Billy coerced you into marriage? Remember how it felt like a bear trap? Why shouldn't you be allowed to have fun and feel alive? Wouldn't you love to be dancing?

"I don't know. I want to be good." I knew she was beginning to weaken.

You know Billy will take advantage of any female opportunities that come his way. Remember how popular he was in high school? You saw how much he still flirted even after you were going steady. Do you think he'd be sitting here telling pretty girls that he was married?

"But I won't have sex. I will stay faithful to Billy in that way and not cheat on him."

That would be an easy promise to keep. Just like she had in high school, Bettie would kiss and neck and do everything but "it." Besides, she had already learned that once a man starts having sex with you, the foreplay goes away and it becomes a race towards penetration and his climax. Not having sex would be far more fun.

She started slipping her wedding ring into her purse and allowed Goldie to introduce her with her maiden name. It didn't take long before Bettie and her new friends were meeting men for unchaperoned activities like roller-coaster rides at Playland-at-the-Beach, bike rides in Golden Gate Park, and pinball at the Fun Center on Powell and Market in the downtown.

On some nights, Bettie and her friends would hang out with enlisted men. They would dance to jukeboxes and walk down Market and Kearney streets to peer in the windows of tattoo parlors. One time, Goldie had to beg her drunken date not to tattoo her name on his bicep.

Sometimes the men, upon hearing their accents, would call them Southern Belles. Bettie and Goldie would look at each other and laugh, knowing that the rich society matrons of Tennessee would be horrified to hear them given such a title. It would just be more proof that the Yankees didn't know a thing.

Occasionally, her friends would go out to a bar just off the Embarcadero, south of Market. Bettie knew that those bars were frequented by the longshoremen and defense workers. They made good money, but she preferred the temporary and transient nature that military men offered. Besides, like me, she loved the posture of a warrior.

On those evenings, she would stay home and read, or visit a movie. One film, *Since you Went Away*, was about the temptations faced by the girls left at home. Bettie felt less guilty knowing that she wasn't alone in her misbehavior.

Bettie and Goldie's favorite place was the St. Francis Hotel on Union Square. Frequented by officers, who called it "the Frantic," it offered non-stop dancing in the Mural Room.

The Mural Room was stunning with a painted ceiling and murals of romantic stories covering the walls. But to Bettie, the best part was the gigantic dance floor located in the center of the room. At one end was a stage where touring Big Bands played. A raised platform wrapped around the other three sides for dining and drinking. Bettie felt like she was dancing on a stage with the audience watching from their tables.

"I love having the tables out of the way," Bettie said to a young pilot as he took her hand and led her to the dance floor.

"Sure beats bumping into them like you do at juke-joints," he said and the pair were soon breathless from jitterbugging.

Although those young people on the dance floor didn't realize it, they were engaging in a type of ecstatic dance invented by the Maenads, followers of Dionysus, the God of Wine and Revelry. They would abandon themselves to rhythm, dance themselves into a trance, and induce a wild delirium to get outside of themselves. They intuitively knew that sustained intensity produced ecstasy.

The jitterbug provided the same purpose. The welcoming swing beat, the athletic movements, the swirling vortexes of spins and turns, made the dancers feel connected to each other. It provided a ritualized way of dealing with stress. Jitterbugging helped the dancers overcome their fear of the war and a future filled with uncertainty, including death.

Bettie was an incredible dancer. "It's probably the best gift Billy ever gave me," she told Goldie. Bettie was in demand all night and rarely sat down.

Back in their apartment, Goldie would ask her for lessons in hopes that she could become as popular. They bought records by Glenn Miller, the Andrew Sisters, Duke Ellington, Count Basie, and Tommy Dorsey. The sounds of swing emanated from their apartment. Angry knocking on the wall and ceiling from their neighbors reminded them to turn it down.

Bettie and Goldie loved how San Francisco, a cosmopolitan port city, let them leave their past behind. No one needed to know about their poverty or shameful family. In California, they had great jobs, money, and could reinvent themselves.

In their studio apartment, they shared a double bed, just like they had as children––except, back then, their little sister, Joyce, would be with them too. Laying there, cozily together in the dark, they would marvel at their new lives.

"The dress I bought today is scandalous. It barely hits my knees," said Goldie. The two of them laughed. "The teachers at school would measure my hemlines with a ruler whenever I tried to shorten them by tucking the extra fabric above my belt. Remember how you used to sew my clothes from old feed sacks?"

"Dresses for you and Joyce, shorts for Jimmie and Jack, and aprons for mama. Thank goodness for those sewing classes at the Community Center," said Bettie.

"You were always over there. You couldn't have been sewing all that time."

"No, I would escape there. Free from the demands and chaos. I would read or do my homework. Anything to look busy and have a reason to not go home."

"Well, I'm happy to have you here with me now. This feels like home," said Goldie before drifting off to sleep.

#

One work day, as she was a typing, a handsome older gentleman entered. "Good day, Sir," Bettie said, standing at her desk.

She saw his eyes travel up and down her figure, but his tone was respectful as he said, "What do we have here? A little Georgia Peach?"

"Tennessee. I grew up in Nashville," said Bettie.

"Lovely," he said and pulled his card out of his wallet. "Art Grayson," he said, handing it to her. "I'm here to see Mr. Roberts about an order." Bettie looked down at the appointment book and heard him quietly add, "but I'd like to talk with you when I'm finished."

"Oh, okay," she said and buzzed him into her boss' office. After he was gone, she read the card, "Art Grayson, president of Hollywood Commerce Motion Pictures." Bettie felt her heart leap.

Maybe you are about to be discovered. Just like Lana Turner sitting at the soda fountain in Hollywood.

"Oh, I hope so. Can you imagine if it were all this easy?" Bettie said. Her legs bounced under her desk in excitement as she waited for Mr. Grayson to come out of the meeting.

My prediction was right. Mr. Grayson offered Bettie an opportunity to model for newspaper ads. Her first assignment was to pose for a window washing company. The modeling session took about an hour, and she had to pretend to be a delighted housewife staring at her sparkling windows.

That night, she told Goldie all about it as they made dinner on a hotplate. "I just love the way it feels to be in front of the camera. It's like I know exactly how I look from the outside. Even when he directed me, I could see a picture of myself in my mind and get right into the position he wanted."

"I'm not surprised," said Goldie. "You were always so good at posing. Remember how we used to play that movie star game in the orphanage?" She asked as she fried up some Spam.

"That was the only thing that made that year bearable. I was eleven, how old were you?" Bettie tore some leaves from a head of iceberg lettuce and rinsed them.

"Seven. Remember how we would sit in a circle and one girl would get in the center and strike a pose? We had to guess the movie star from the pose and facial expression," recalled Goldie. "You were always the best. I remember feeling so proud that you were my big sister."

"Aww," said Bettie, squeezing Goldie's shoulder. "Maybe you are right. Maybe that silly posing game is why I felt so natural today."

She popped a cucumber slice in her mouth and chewed it thoughtfully.

"What are you thinking about?" Goldie asked as she took two plates out of the cupboard.

"I'm just trying to imagine what it must have felt like for Momma to give us up to the orphanage."

"She always told us she never wanted girls anyways," said Goldie as she slapped the Spam slices onto each plate. "She was probably thrilled to be rid of you, me, and Joycie."

"I don't know. She was so full of pride. It must have been humiliating to admit she was too broke to take care of her kids."

"I've never told a soul about it—have you?" Goldie studied Bettie's face and held her breath.

"Never, not even Billy. But if we are this ashamed, can you imagine how poor Momma must have felt?" She winced and began building two salads on the plates.

"Poor Momma, poor, poor Momma. I don't know why you always stick up for her. She isn't a nice person, and she sure never treats you very well."

Bettie pursed her lips, thinking. "The older I get, the more I understand her. Married to a hound-dog like Daddy, broke and pregnant all the time." Bettie carried the two plates to the table and Goldie followed with glasses of milk and silverware. They sat down and began to eat.

Bettie reminisced, "I don't know if you were old enough to remember, but when she was eight-months pregnant with Jack, Daddy locked her out of the house in the pouring rain."

"Why?" Goldie asked, her eyes wide.

"Why do you think?" Bettie asked in an irked tone. "What did they always fight about?"

"Sex and money." Goldie bit her bottom lip "Don't tell me he expected her to have sex with him at eight-months?"

"Yep. I'll never forget how sick I felt to my stomach. William was gone, and Jimmie and I just stood there, wanting to let her in, but terrified of Daddy. Then you burst into sobs, so there I was, comforting you inside and listening to Momma sobbing outside."

"How did it end?" Goldie looked ill.

"Momma had to agree to have sex. That bastard opened the door, grabbed her wrist and dragged her straight to the bedroom. She was soaking wet, and he didn't even care." Bettie shook her head.

"I'll bet she ended up with one of her colds. It seemed like she was always sick."

"Sick in body and sick in spirit." Bettie lifted her hands in surrender. "Now can you see why I always give her the benefit of the doubt? No one should have to live the way she did."

"It's like God was punishing her for being a woman. Cursing her with fertility and a rotten man."

"And no money, and no way to earn it because she always had to deal with her kids."

Goldie reached for Bettie's hand. "I pray God doesn't curse us like that."

"Me too," whispered Bettie.

6

Star Search

Bettie had more opportunities for modeling. Her natural smile and buoyant attitude shined through, no matter what product she was selling. Art was a perfect gentleman and seemed genuinely interested in her success. He never made a pass at her, and this made Bettie even more relaxed during the photo shoots.

One day, Art took Bettie out for a fancy lunch. Bettie wore her best navy-blue jersey dress and a red cardigan against the Pacific chill. "Great news, Bettie," he said as he pulled out her chair at the table.

"What is it, sir," she asked, putting her napkin in her lap.

"I sent some of your pictures to 20th Century Fox," Bettie felt a rush of anticipation. "And they want you to come in for a screen test."

"What? Me? A screen-test?" Bettie squealed and other patrons glanced over at their table.

"It's for next Monday. We are going to fly down to L.A. Can you get the day off?" He asked.

"Yes, of course. Oh my gosh, I get to fly?" Bettie felt like her face was going to split from her smile. "Thank you so much. Thank you, Mr. Grayson."

I was thrilled at this development and had nothing to do with it. Well, I imagine having my presence inside her made her sexier and more outgoing than usual, but she got it all on her own.

#

The flight to L.A. had a bit too much drama for my taste. As Art and Bettie waited to board, they heard a woman's voice shouting. "No, you don't, you dog!"

Bettie saw a middle-aged woman running towards them, rage on her face. The gate opened, and Art told Bettie to go ahead and join the others walking across the tarmac to the plane. He held out his hands towards the crazed woman. "Honey, calm down. This isn't what you think."

"She's half your age. You think you can jump on a plane and have a fling? You think I don't know what this is all about?" She hit him on the chest.

The loud speaker announced the flight and warned passengers to board.

"It's a screen test. That's all it is. She's my client. I told you about her. That's Bettie." He placated, backing towards the gate.

"No. I forbid you to go. Those legs—I know what you like. You're not going to get away with this." She started to pull on his coat and tried to drag him back.

"I'll be back this evening." He pushed her clutching claws off of him. "We can talk then." Disengaging himself, Art started to run for the plane. Bettie watched from the plane's staircase as he hurdled the closed gate and ran for the stairs. She wanted to cheer.

Stay quiet. Don't talk to Art about this. Pretend like nothing has happened.

I had seen the look of venom on the wife's face and feared a Hera-inspired revenge. In the Greek world, mortals always feared Ares and thought he was the most unlikeable. Au contraire. Nothing is scarier than Hera in a rage. Men like Ares can always be controlled with seduction. It doesn't take much to move their brain into their little head. A wife is someone an Aphrodite should always steer clear of.

I hoped Bettie hadn't created a mess that would get in the way of her burgeoning career.

#

The short flight to L.A. was marked by tense silence. Bettie and I felt terrible for Art. He had been such a respectful, upstanding guy that it seemed unfair that his wife suspected him of cheating. Bettie wanted to broach the subject, but I warned her again to stay silent.

Once they arrived in L.A., a car was waiting to take them to Fox Studio. Art distractedly introduced Bettie to the stylist and assured her she would be in good hands. Pulling Bettie aside, he said, "Look, there is this thing called the Casting Couch. Have you heard of it?"

Innocent, Bettie shook her head. I knew exactly what it was, and I had fully intended to encourage Bettie to use it to get ahead. I was disappointed to hear Art continue, "Old guys, my age and worse, are going to offer to take you out to dinner, or to see the latest show at the Pantages Theater. Don't do it. They will make all kinds of promises, but they just want to get you into bed."

"I'll tell them I'm married," said Bettie. She always wore her ring at work and went by Mrs. Neal.

"That won't bother them. Most of them are too. So just say no if they ask you out," Art concluded with a stern look.

"Of course. I mean, no. I'll say no."

"Good girl." Art patted her on her shoulder. "Listen, I've got to go home and deal with my wife."

"What? But you're my agent, aren't you going to stay and speak for me?" Bettie pleaded.

Art rubbed the back of his neck. "That was my intention, but I've got to go. You've got this, just be yourself and smile." He handed Bettie some money to pay for lunch and the ticket for her return trip that evening. With a final pat of reassurance, he left.

The stylist ushered Bettie into the backroom. The hair dresser and make-up artist conspired to make Bettie look like a young Joan Crawford. Bettie watched the transformation in horror as they bushed out her black hair, thickened her eyebrows, and made her mouth look double its natural size with blood-red lipstick.

I kept trying to reassure her. I knew if she felt ugly, she wouldn't perform well.

It's okay. Your personality will shine through. You can win anyone over with your smile. It's fine. Don't worry.

But, to be honest, I didn't think she stood a chance. She looked like a horrible caricature. Besides, Joan Crawford was about as polar opposite in temperament as sweet Bettie. This was before Mommy Dearest, but Crawford had a reputation for ruthlessness since her early days at the studio.

As predicted by Art, a studio exec found his way to the dressing room. He stood watching the make-up artist apply the finishing touches and then sent her away with a sharp tilt of his head towards the door. "Hey Doll, you look terrific." He rested his hands on Bettie's shoulders and met her eyes in the mirror. "I was hoping I could take you out for dinner after your screen test."

Bettie felt a shiver of revulsion at the feel of his fingers kneading her shoulders. With a deep breath and a huge smile, she said, "My husband is risking his life in the Pacific, fighting for our country. It wouldn't be right to betray him." She swallowed and smiled brighter. "Even though I would love to go out with you."

Bettie felt his hands transform into claws as he leaned down and whispered in her ear, "You'll regret it."

Bettie didn't regret not going to bed with the old creep. However, she always wondered if that was why she didn't get a call back for the screen test. The same man who had approached her was one of the judges in the testing room. As he watched her pose and walk for the camera, he leaned back in his chair with his hands crossed on his belly and let his boredom and disinterest telegraph itself. This, on top of her Crawford looks, and Art's abandonment, made Bettie nervous and uncharacteristically shy. It was a fiasco from start to finish.

"We'll call you," the exec said as an assistant took Bettie out of the room to clean off her make up.

She sat quietly in the chair like a mannequin. I could feel the depression flooding Bettie's body so I tried to cheer her up.

Come on, let's spend the next few hours exploring Hollywood before our flight.

Bettie rallied. As soon as she could, she left the studio and hopped into a cab. "Take me to 1451 Cahuenga Boulevard," she directed.

"The Hollywood Canteen," said the driver. "Hoping to spy a star?" He was an older man in his fifties and he smelled like garlic.

"Bette Davis, she's my favorite actress. I've loved her ever since *Dark Victory*." Bettie continued with her star-struck voice. "She organized the Canteen to support the soldiers. I volunteer at the USO myself, in San Francisco."

The driver eyed her in the rear-view mirror. "I'm sure you provide those boys with a welcome diversion." The taxi stopped in front of the wooden building. The sign, Hollywood Canteen, was written in cursive and the H was lower case. Bettie thought of how much her English teachers would have hated that abuse of writing conventions.

A line of servicemen went around the block. "You know you can't get inside unless you're in uniform," said the driver.

"Oh, no, I didn't realize that." Bettie stared out the window and had second thoughts about hanging out with all those servicemen by herself.

"Never mind, just drive me back to Hollywood Blvd."

In the end, Bettie ended up having lunch at Coffee Dan's. She flew back to San Francisco alone, on the evening plane, never having seen a star and certain she would never become one herself.

#

Back home, Bettie fell into a funk. She stopped going out with Goldie and her friends and sat home alone in the evenings. To comfort herself, she began bingeing on donuts and sweets. It didn't take long before she put on 20 pounds.

She stood in front of the mirror, fixing her hair for work. She had been avoiding looking at herself from the chest down. She even looked away when walking past The Emporium, a department store whose large windows made a perfect mirror. I hated to see her perfect figure be thrown away in a fit of self-pity.

Come on Bettie. Get it together. Feel how tight your waistband feels? Look at that roll. See how the fabric strains across your hips? If you don't get this under control you'll turn into a heifer.

I know it was harsh, but I had to talk some sense into her.

What about Billy? Won't he be disappointed to see you looking like this? Remember, the girls at home need to mind their looks for the war effort. We don't want to harm soldier morale.

"Who knows what Billy wants? He is always so suspicious in his letters. You would think I was the soldier and needing to write a Behavior Report, instead of him. He'd probably be thrilled to see me in one of those dresses the fat women wear in Hawaii—what did Jimmie say they were called?"

Muumuu.

Bettie's brother, Jimmie, had told her about the loose colorful dress in a letter that he included with a package containing a genuine grass skirt from Hawaii. Bettie had been thrilled to receive the skirt with its woven band, adorned with real cowry shells, but now kept it in the back of her closet while she ate her feelings.

You know you want more from life than this. Don't let one sleazy executive steal your dreams of stardom. Besides, even with the weight, you notice that men are still looking at you. Use your power, don't throw it away because of one set back.

"Right." Bettie tucked her shirt tightly into her skirt and pinched an inch over the waistline. She stuck her tongue out at herself in the mirror. "I'm bored with myself and I should be going out and having fun. I'll get back into shape." She went to the box where she kept her stash of snack foods and picked it up. "No more." She marched down to the dumpster and tossed it inside. On the ground lay a newspaper. I made the wind blow it open to an ad.

"Become a model. Enroll in our 3-week course and learn how to pose, walk, and win contracts." Bettie read it aloud and looked at the picture of the smiling girl. "I could do that. I already have some experience. Maybe this class will give me some insider tips." Kneeling down, she picked up the newspaper and tucked it under her arm. Her heart felt light for the first time since the screen test.

#

Bettie felt like the modeling course was a bust. "$100 to learn how to walk with a book on my head," she complained to Goldie. However, I knew that the seeds for her future had been sown. She was never a drinker, but now she shunned cigarettes after learning that they caused wrinkles and damaged the skin. She ate fresh, natural foods and began doing calisthenics. She soon shed 20 pounds and felt like her usual upbeat self.

She got a new job, modeling fur coats and doing basic secretarial work for Geary Furriers. She fell in love with ermine.

"It's better than mink—so silky and sensuous," she would tell customers in her sweet Southern drawl, as she looked over her shoulder and caressed the fur. Many a sale was made after her performance.

One of her daily rituals included letter writing. She had four letters going at once: Billy Neal, of course, and her brothers. Every Saturday, Bettie would start a letter to each man and add a paragraph to it each day of the week. She would post them Friday morning on her way to work. She loved receiving answers, even though they were heavily blacked out by the censors.

Bettie didn't realize it, but I, the Goddess of Love, noticed a growing distance and coldness in her letters to her husband. Bettie saved her exciting stories of mishaps and adventures that she and Goldie had for her brothers. To Billy Neal, she remarked upon the weather and the local events in San Francisco. Distance had not made her heart grow fonder. I wondered how Billy felt.

#

Bettie was thrilled to learn from Art Grayson that he had received a telegram from Warner Brothers inviting Bettie for a screen test. She felt nervous, but confident and looked forward to it.

Her optimism vanished when, the next day, she received a letter from Billy Neal saying he was on his way home from the South Pacific.

"I shouldn't have married him in the first place," Bettie said to herself. "He tricked me with his talk of dying and how I owed it to him and my country."

I felt encouraged by her thoughts.

You are 22 years old, an independent woman with her own job and own apartment. You don't need a man. Do you really want to go back to Nashville and be a housewife?

"No. I dread seeing him. I feel like I am an entirely different person than I was when I got married."

Then end it, send him a letter and then you won't even have to see him again.

"I can't send him a 'Dear John' letter. That wouldn't be kind." Bettie punched a pillow and paced the room.

Are you sure? You know how persuasive Billy can be. Better send a letter.

I knew that seeing Billy face to face, after two years apart, would weaken her resolve.

"No, I will tell him in person, when he gets home. I'll tell him it's over," she said as she slammed her fist down on his letter with conviction.

The scene with Billy didn't go well, as I predicted.

#

Bettie met Billy at the docks wearing a new red dress with padded sleeves and a thin belt. Her heart melted at the way he ran towards her, grabbed her, and gave her a deep French kiss. All the longing and missing of the past two years was in that kiss.

"Ah, Baby. It feels so good to have you in my arms again," Billy said, kissing the side of her head as they walked towards the bus stop. On the ride back to the apartment, Bettie asked questions and prompted Billy to do most of the talking while she debated in her head about breaking up with him. Goldie had agreed to spend the night at a friend's place to give them privacy.

Once in the apartment, Billy pulled her into bed, and Bettie laughed at his enthusiasm. Bettie tried not to compare Billy's kisses with the other boys she had been necking with. Those make-out sessions were slow and sensuous, and the lack of consummation meant the boys spent time pleasing Bettie instead of themselves. Sex with Billy was hurried and frantic. Bettie didn't find much pleasure in it, but she told herself that it made sense since they had been apart for so long.

Billy took a nap, and Bettie got up and made some coffee. "What should I do?" she asked.

You've welcomed him home, now do what you planned and break it off.

Billy was provincial. I had big plans for Bettie, and she couldn't accomplish them with a husband hanging like an albatross around her neck. I practiced various good-bye speeches with her.

When Billy woke up, the first thing he did was reach for Bettie. "Let me show you again how much I missed you."

"We need to talk," Bettie said, sitting on the bed beside him.

Every man dreads those words. Billy got out of bed, and pulled on his pants and shirt. He crossed his arms across his chest, and with his legs braced, stood about three feet away from her. "About what?"

"While you've been gone, I have enjoyed life here in San Francisco––working, living with Goldie in this apartment and I feel that we don't have much in common anymore," Bettie looked down and tensed for his response.

"Enjoyed life? How nice for you. While I was in Okinawa, ducking grenades and watching my buddies die, you were having a grand old time." He looked around the studio, which Bettie and Goldie had decorated with bright colors and potted plants. "I'll bet this was a popular flop house."

"What?" Bettie looked up, confused.

"Flop house. I'll bet every sailor on leave knew this address and you spread your legs for all of them." He shouted, "My parents warned me not to marry white trash. I always defended you. I should have known that you were a slut." He threw his beer bottle. The glass shattered and brown foam ran down the wall, puddling on the carpet.

Bettie stared at the broken glass and her heart raced. Inside, she felt like a little girl huddling in fear at her Daddy's latest outburst. She wanted to flee, and she wanted to hide. She sat motionless. I could feel her trembling. The rage that poured off of Billy frightened me too. An Ares man could be unpredictable when provoked.

Just apologize. Agree to whatever he wants so he doesn't hit you.

"Am I right?" Billy walked to the bed and towered over Bettie.

"What? No, Billy, I have been faithful to you. I never betrayed you," Bettie pleaded.

"Bullshit. You slept with every man that looked at you." Bettie sputtered denials, but Billy continued. "Your little sashay, swinging that perfect ass as you walk down the street. Your inviting smile—once those were for me, but now you give yourself away."

Bettie started crying. "No, that isn't true. I love you."

"Love me? I thought you loved your life and wanted to leave me," Billy shouted as he paced the tiny living room.

"No, I don't. I'm sorry. I was wrong, I just missed you and you've been gone so long that...I don't know, I thought it might be easier to part." She took a deep breath and met his eyes, "I want to make this marriage work."

Try and seduce him. Distract him with your body.

She stood and started to hug him but he twisted out of her grasp. Bettie followed him, reaching out her arms but not touching him. "I am your wife, your faithful wife, and I will follow you, wherever you want to go."

Billy grabbed her chin, and she stiffened at the hate she saw in his eyes. "Damn right. You are MY wife. You are going to stop whoring around and behave yourself," he dropped his hand and shoved her away. "Nashville," Billy said. He panted with anger as he put on his socks and shoes. "We're going home to my folks. Better give your notice at work and on this flop house." He grabbed his coat off the chair, glared at her over his shoulder and left, slamming the front door behind him.

I felt dread wash through Bettie's body as she sunk back down on the couch.

Going back to Tennessee will be a mistake. It will be easier to escape him here, in California. Pack a bag. Call Goldie. Let's hide at one of her girlfriend's apartments. Maybe he'll get frustrated and just go home.

"No. He is right, and I am wrong. I deserve to be punished. I cheated on Billy, maybe not with sex, but in every other way. Leaving him would make his accusations true."

Who cares? You have a new life in California. No one knows you or him. He can talk bad about you all he wants in Nashville. It won't affect you out here.

"Maybe, no matter how much I try, I'll always just be my father's daughter."

What are you talking about? You are nothing like your Daddy.

"I can't seem to keep it in my pants, can I? He destroyed his marriage and my mother chasing sex. How am I different?" Her heart raced and her breath came in staccato pants.

Take a deep breath.

Bettie obeyed.

Now another. That's good. Count ten deep breaths.

I could feel Bettie's pulse slow as she reined the run-away horse of her emotions under control.

Listen to me. You are nothing like your father. Your father seduced adolescents. He abused his wife. He hurt people with his sexuality.

"And I hurt Billy."

Not even close. You felt pressured by him into a marriage that you didn't want. Then you necked with a few boys while he was away. You didn't get pregnant from another man and try and pass the baby off as your own, doing that would make you like your Daddy.

"I need to redeem myself. I will become a good wife."

You know this is a mistake.

Bettie wouldn't listen to me. She repressed me and busied herself cleaning the beer off the wall and picking up the broken glass. By the time Billy returned to the apartment at 2 a.m., Bettie was packed and ready to leave for Nashville.

She had three letters: one for her boss at the fur shop, telling him she had to move home; one for Goldie with money for the utilities; and the last to Art Grayson. She thanked him for his support of her modeling and acting career, informed him that she would not be able to attend the screen test with Warner Brothers, and asked him not to contact her again.

"I don't want any temptation to come back here instead of dedicating myself to my marriage," she thought as she sealed the envelope.

#

Back home in Nashville, Bettie got a job at the Office of Price Administration. Billy went back to work with his dad at the car dealership. Some evenings, Bettie would stand on the front porch, and I could feel how much she dreaded entering the house.

Most nights, after doing the dishes and helping Mrs. Neal straighten up the house, Bettie would go into the room she shared with Billy and read. Sitting in the living room and listening to the radio felt like torture. She couldn't forget how his parents hadn't wanted him to get married because she was trash.

Besides, when she did make an effort to sit with the family, Billy just brooded or snapped angry retorts. Conversation was stilted and even his parents gave up. A heavy silence settled over the house and everyone walked on egg shells.

Gone were Billy's dancing days. Instead, he stayed home and his eyes followed every move Bettie made. She took to dressing more conservatively because any outfit that was mildly fashionable provoked his ire. He picked her up every day from work, even though she could have walked home. He didn't want to give her the freedom of going out for drinks with her colleagues. She had done that once, when they first returned to Nashville, and Billy met her at the door in an explosion of rage.

Her brother, Jack, invited her out for a night on the town, but Billy vetoed it—accusing her of having round heels.

"I'm going out with my brother! Do you really think I would be misbehaving in front of him?" She asked.

Billy barked a skeptical laugh. "As if any of you Pages have integrity. You had Goldie catting around with you in California. I don't trust any relative of yours to act as a chaperone."

Bettie didn't understand the change that had come over Billy; he was so different from the man she had married. I knew what had happened, but I couldn't explain it to her in a way that she could understand. Before the war, Billy had been similar to Eros, my son, the God of Love. He was compassionate, loving, and full of life. However, whatever had happened during the war had turned Billy towards Thantos, the God of Death. He was now filled with anger, violence and aggression.

There was nothing Bettie could do to change him, but that didn't keep her from trying.

She tried to share his interests and discuss the newest car models coming out of Detroit.

"I love the new Buick Super." She pointed to the picture of the green automobile in her magazine. "This stamped grill, and the torpedo shaped fenders. Just beautiful. Isn't your Dad going to carry them?"

"He carries him. He's not an idiot," snapped Billy and pushed the magazine away.

"I was just wondering because you used to love to drive the latest models." Bettie watched his face, saw his anger rising, but stumbled on. "...and now you are still driving that black one from before the war."

"I'm sure you'd love a Super, driving around town and getting all that attention. It must be horrible for you to have to be a humble wife, instead of a flashy flirt."

Bettie tried to keep the peace and leave Billy alone. But, no matter how much they fought, he would always reach for her in the night. Sex became a duty that she dreaded. Billy seemed obsessed with getting her pregnant. He promised that as soon as she was, he would get a low-interest Veteran loan and buy them a house. Bettie wondered why he didn't use the G.I. Bill to go to college, but she kept her mouth shut. She was learning to keep her opinions to herself.

As long as she wasn't pregnant, Billy would let her work. She knew that once she had that first baby she would be trapped. Every month, she held her breath, but her flow always arrived, right on time. Billy took her infertility personally, an affront to his Ares manliness. He accused Bettie of being sterile because she must have caught V.D. while he was at sea. He accused her of sabotaging his performance with her lack of enthusiasm.

I could feel her vibrant life force dimming with each argument and accusation. I tried to counter her depression with dire warnings and dreams of freedom.

You have to leave him. The day you get pregnant your life will become the same as your Momma's. Don't you want more? You gave up that screen test for him. Why are you willing to give up your spirit?

"I don't know what I can do."

Leave him. You tried to be a good wife, but you must see that Billy has changed.

"Even if I wanted to, how could I get away? He watches me like a hawk."

Have you told your Momma? Maybe she can help you.

"Are you kidding? She never has any money and there is always a new creepy boyfriend to replace the last one. Going to her would be jumping out of the frying pan and into the fire."

You have at least $100 in your suitcase. It's a miracle you could hide it from Billy. What if you called Jack? Maybe he could help you escape one night, take you to the Greyhound so you can disappear.

"I don't want to get a divorce. It would be such a scene."

No, don't bother with that. Just get away from him.

Bettie called her brother Jack from work the next day. He agreed to help her and they made a plan. Billy had one tie to his old life. Every Wednesday night, he would go play poker with his high school buddies. He usually came home drunk. Bettie always welcomed Wednesdays because it was the one night of the week Billy didn't want sex and would tumble into bed and sleep.

"This Wednesday. I'll hide my bags in the bushes and then creep outside. Pick me up at 4:00 a.m."

7

Freedom

With her savings, Bettie set off for Miami Beach. A ticket to California cost too much, and she was afraid Billy would follow her. She didn't know a soul in Florida, but she wanted to see the Atlantic Ocean.

In Miami Beach, she found a room in a boarding house. Every day, we scoured the help-wanted section of the newspaper.

Bettie had an impressive resume with four different jobs, and a glowing letter of referral from her boss at the furrier shop. I knew she would have no trouble securing work. I just wanted to make sure it was interesting and provided opportunities for my kind of entertainment.

Wanted: Efficient typist/secretary open to adventure. This sounds intriguing--you should call the number.

"It sounds kind off fishy. What kind of adventure is there in secretarial work?

Call it and find out.

Bettie called the number and went to a hat shop for the interview. She immediately liked the husband and wife who had placed the ad. As I expected, they were impressed with her work experience. The wife immediately offered her a job as a stenographer.

"I can start right away," said Bettie.

Ask about the adventure.

The husband took over the interview and revealed, "My business, a mahogany furniture business, is in Port-au-Prince."

"Is that nearby?" Bettie asked.

The couple laughed. "It's in Haiti. The country that shares the island of Hispaniola with the Dominican Republic, down in the Caribbean," he explained.

"Near Cuba?" Bettie had seen pictures of the movie stars and socialites frolicking in the pools and dancing in the casinos of Havana.

"Cuba is about 50 miles west."

Bettie's heart quickened with anticipation. "Live in the Tropics? That sounds fun!"

The couple looked relieved, "It's four months. My husband is going to liquidate his business down there, so we can focus on our hat store here in Miami."

"We will pay salary, plus plane fare, and expenses," he added.

"I'll start packing," said Bettie as she signed the contract.

#

It didn't take much for Bettie to get ready to leave. She packed her one suitcase and flew down to Port-au-Prince that week with the husband.

He explained the society of Haiti on the flight. "There is a strong class division in the country. The upper class consists mostly of mulattoes, who are well educated and speak both French and English. The lower class are blacks, mostly farmers and laborers."

"Do they have Jim Crow laws between the mulattoes and the blacks?" Bettie asked in confusion.

"No, they don't need them. Culture keeps the rules in place," he said.

"Sounds like California. They don't have Jim Crow, like Tennessee, but the military and the workplaces were still pretty segregated. When we went out, there were certain parts of town for blacks that we didn't venture into."

"The oppressed are getting restless," he said. "It is only a matter of time before things erupt. That's why I'm moving my business out of Haiti." He paused, lost in thought, then continued with an angry tone. "It's just like in the States. The blacks are sick of being treated like second-class citizens, and I don't blame them. You heard about the race riots in Detroit and Harlem, didn't you?"

"Yes, that was terrible. A marine told me there was one in Guam too––between American black and white soldiers."

"Can you blame them? The war was about fighting racist Nazi Germany and protecting democracy. We asked those boys to fight and then treat them like dirt in our own land of the free."

Bettie had never heard a white man criticize the racial problems of America. She spent the rest of the flight thinking about what she had seen in Tennessee and California in an entirely different way. She questioned what she had been taught to assume.

#

Port-au-Prince was filled with French colonial architecture, tropical plants, and open-air squares. The two-story buildings, with large balconies and wrought iron railings, reminded her of New Orleans. Turquoise, pink, yellow and blue homes climbed the green mountains. Everywhere she went there were new smells––spices, tropical plants, burning charcoal, and fritay stands on the corner selling fried pork or fish. The sound of bells and hawkers outside of the casinos mingled with the Haitian Creole spoken by the poor.

Her job at the furniture store was easy. With her sunny disposition and friendliness, Bettie quickly made a group of friends. Fellow ex-pats, they were all interested in exploring the country. One day, they rode mules 4,000 feet up Massif du Nord to see the Citadelle la Ferriere.

Bettie, happy to get off the mule, read to her friends from the guidebook, "The Citadelle is a fortress built by Henry Cristophe, a leader in the war of Haitian Independence who proclaimed himself King Henry and ruled from 1811-1820." From the mountain top, Bettie pointed down towards Cap-Hatien. "That is the former capital of Haiti and called the Paris of the Antilles."

Bettie loved how the white colonial architecture contrasted with the rusted tin roofs and tropical paint colors. I loved her openness and spirit of adventure. The only thing missing was for me was sex.

That missing piece came the next day as she was laying on the white sand beach in a red swim-suit she had sewn herself. It was a bikini, something no one wore in the States, but was popular in the Islands. Her black hair was wet from swimming in the warm turquoise waters and the sun tanned her skin.

A handsome young man in a brief swim suit approached her. "*Bonjour*, may I join you? My name is Francois."

Bettie smiled, sat up, and made room for him on her towel. "How did you know I spoke English?"

He sat beside her. "The bikini made me think you were French. But as soon as I saw your smile, I knew you were American."

"Why?" As she flirted, I admired his muscular arms and pectoral muscles.

"Your teeth. You have beautiful, straight, American teeth." He smiled and leaned towards her. Francois was a mulatto with beautiful amber eyes and full lips. I immediately took notice, and Bettie did too.

Francois invited Bettie out to lunch, and they ate fritay while sitting on a park bench. Bettie found herself captivated by his lilting, island-French accent. He explained that he had grown up in Haiti, and his father was a manager of one of the US Standard Fruit banana plantations. He had grown up attending Company schools and was currently a clerk at the U.S. Embassy.

"Would you like to go out tonight, *Cherie*?" He purred and leaned into her shoulder.

Bettie felt her toes curl. "Yes, that would be lovely." *I could see by the look in his eyes that he wanted to have sex with her. I spent the remainder of the day encouraging her.*

If he wants to sleep with you, then go for it.

"I don't know. I still feel bad about Billy...and we are still married."

Billy? You can't seriously be thinking about him. You should have written him a Dear John letter and saved yourself months of misery. You paid your dues and tried to be a good wife. Now you deserve to have some fun.

"I just keep thinking that I should have worked harder. Maybe I could have saved the marriage."

You did try. It is impossible for you to get unhappy enough to make him happy. That isn't how it works. Billy needs to make himself happy. You need to worry about yourself, and I think Francois will make you very happy.

Eventually Bettie capitulated and Francois did not disappoint. Having known only Billy, Bettie was surprised at all the attention he paid to her. Kissing behind her ear, caressing her sides, licking behind her knees, and reveling in her scent. He was a slow, attentive lover and adored her body. Throughout their love making, he whispered compliments in French and English.

Bettie felt sensations she had never felt before. Instead of Billy's rush to finish, Francois took his time, and Bettie orgasmed for her first time while making love. With Billy, she had only come when he used his finger, and as their relationship deteriorated, that had started to feel like he was scrubbing a pot instead of trying to give her pleasure. As her affair with Francois continued, she discovered all the amazing pleasures her body was capable of. It reminded me of the delight I felt discovering Ares as a lover after having known only my husband Hephaestus.

Her pleasure was multiplied by Francois' love of dancing. Merengue was the craze, called the Latin march dance, and it was easy to learn. Bettie quickly mastered the Latin hip movement, created by straightening one knee to send the hip out before shifting weight to the other leg. The dance started in closed position with her arms on his shoulders and his on her waist. It was filled with spins, during which the dancers kept their eyes on their partner's face, turning their head only at the last minute.

Flirty and passionate, the merengue fit Bettie and me to a T. My favorite move was when both dancers would hold hands with their arms straight and below their waists, then they would slowly raise their arms until they were clasped above their heads, all the while holding eye contact. It reminded me of the best moments of making love.

One evening, Francois picked Bettie up from the furniture shop. "I have a treat for you," he said, taking Bettie by the hand. "You need to go home and change into all black and wear pants with tennis shoes.

"Sounds exciting. Where are we going?" Bettie cooed.

"I am going to take you into the woods to see a secret Vodou ritual by the locals, it is important we not get caught."

Bettie changed, and they crept into the woods. Careful to stay hidden by the trees, they peered out into a dirt clearing. Bettie felt the drum beat inside her core, a rhythmic ponding that echoed her heartbeat. There was a metallic chiming sound. Bettie thought it might have been coming from a steel drum, but she couldn't be sure. Singers chanted words she didn't understand in an "ahhh-eee" sound that undulated up and down and held the same tempo.

"Are they worshipping the devil?" She whispered.

"No, although sometimes Christians like to say they are. Vodou religion is a combination of West African beliefs with a little bit of Catholicism mixed in. It comes from the slaves that were brought here for the French plantations. Vodou believes that everything is spirit. We humans are spirits that inhabit the visible, material world, but the unseen world is populated by *Iwa, myste, anvizib, zanji*."

"What are those?"

"Spirits, mysteries, the invisibles, angels and the spirits of ancestors. See how they are dancing? The drums and the dancing send them into a trance."

Bettie saw male and female dancers with their arms held out to the side, elbows bent, and moving up and down. It would have looked chicken-like, but the dancers also shimmied their shoulders forward and back. They looked down, stuck their butts out and danced flat footed, their feet scuffing the dirt in a grounding motion.

"The trance is the incarnate presence of *Iwa*, the spirit, within the dancer. The ritual is done to restore the balance and energy in relationships between people and the spirits of the unseen world."

Suddenly, a twirling haystack joined the group. Bettie could see there was a dancer beneath the stack holding a pole. He twirled and the hay flew outward. It looked like a whirling dervish as it spun around the clearing. Bettie gasped in surprised delight.

Francois motioned for Bettie to back up and they snuck out of the woods. "That was amazing," she said and gave Francois a hug. "Thank you so much for taking me tonight. It felt magical and powerful. I'll never forget it."

Francois smiled and gave her a kiss. "I'm happy you could appreciate it. I wasn't sure how you might react."

I understood Francois' hesitation. Given Bettie's religious upbringing in the American South, I expected her to be afraid, or at least judgmental of the Vodou dancers. But instead, she respected them. Her open-mindedness reassured me that I was a much better archetype fit for her than rigid Athena would have ever been.

#

The lovers enjoyed a sultry Christmas with each other. Francois gave her a necklace made of shells, and she gave him swim trunks that she sewed herself, modeled after the latest Parisian style. Her job at the furniture store wound to a close, but Francois was able to use his connections to get Bettie a secretarial job at the U.S. Embassy.

The two of them walked along the boardwalk holding hands, but Francois was uncharacteristically silent. Bettie chattered to try and fill the silence.

"I'm so excited about my new job. What do you think I should wear on my first day? I start on Wednesday, so I have a few days off. Maybe we can go on a little trip."

A group of young black men loitered on the boardwalk ahead of them. Francois pulled Bettie with him as they quickly crossed the street. Leaving the oceanfront, he hurried them back towards his home.

"What's the matter?" Bettie asked.

"There is talk of protests. On New Year's Day, a Marxist article came out in the *La Ruche*, the University newspaper, calling for an end of the dictatorship. President Lescot had the writers thrown in prison, here in Port-au-Prince. The black students have been grumbling for some time. This might be the final straw." Francois looked over his shoulder before unlocking his courtyard gate and double-checked that it was secure once they were inside.

Inside the house, he drew the drapes and kept the lights out. I knew all the signs of a man preparing for war, and Bettie felt his anxiety too.

"What are you doing? Are we going to sit here in the dark? What is happening?" She asked.

Francois hushed her. "We have to get you out of Haiti. You don't want to be an American if they win." He rested his forehead on his closed fist. Bettie rubbed his back in growing alarm.

"Win what?"

"Get their demands—oust Lescot from power, hold free elections, institute freedom of the press." He paused and looked at Bettie with fear in his eyes. "Get rid of the American presence in Haiti."

"What about you? Leave with me," she urged.

"I can't. My family, my job—I have to stay here. I am Haitian." He paused and shook his head. "Besides, I don't want to be a black man in America."

"You're right. We could never be together. Marriage between a black man and a white woman is illegal. They call it miscegenation."

They two stared at each other and thought bleakly of all the obstacles society put between them. They kissed, and I could feel their longing for what might have been.

When they stopped, Francois held her hand firmly and said, "But you need to leave. Tomorrow I'm taking you to the airport."

"Alright," she whispered and clung to him. They made desperate, passionate love that night. They both knew they wouldn't see each other again, but pushed the thought aside and lost themselves in each other's bodies.

The next morning, Bettie awoke to the sound of banging pots and shouting, "*Vive la Revolution!*"

She looked out the upstairs window and saw the male students marching by. They wore black pants, white button-down shirts and ties. She thought how civilized everyone looked for a revolution.

Crowds of locals followed the students, farmers marched with upraised machetes, and women banged pots and pans. Teachers, shopkeepers, and office-workers, still dressed in their work clothes, joined the protestors as the entire City shut down on strike.

Francois' face was knitted with tension. He dug through his

drawers and pulled out a pair of drawstring pants and a colorful shirt. "Put this on. Tie up your hair and shove it under this floppy hat."

Bettie got dressed. Francois motioned for her to go down to the garage, which had an alley entrance. He pulled out two bikes.

"They're headed for the U.S. Embassy," he whispered. "We can go the back way to the airport."

They rode through the pot-holed streets. Speeding past shop owners who rushed to close up and join the protest at the Embassy. No one paid them any mind and the mood on the street was as if the crowds were off to join a parade. The light-hearted atmosphere contrasted sharply with Francois's anxiety. Bettie had to peddle as fast as she could to keep up with him and could see the desperation in his eyes when he looked over his shoulder to make sure she was following.

At the airport, Francois bought Bettie a ticket for the next plane out of the country, using his Embassy credentials to get her ahead of the other white foreigners arriving at the airport with panic on their faces.

"*Au revoir, mon amour,*" he said as he gave her one last kiss at the boarding gate.

Crying, Bettie stared out the window as the plane took off and the island of Hispaniola disappeared from sight.

8

Birth of Aphrodite

After Haiti, Bettie returned to Florida and worried about Francois. The media coverage in the U.S. was minimal, but Bettie was able to find out that the protestors she saw passing by her window had been beaten by police when they arrived at the embassy. The leaders were arrested and all protests were banned. Through the national newspaper, Lescot demanded that parents control their youth.

Two days after she left the island, on January 10, Lescot declared martial law and vowed to take any measures necessary to restore order. At a feminist protest that day, he ordered police to shoot into the crowd, killing two protestors. Lescot's cabinet resigned, unable to defend his actions. Additional protests broke out, and police refused to fire into crowds of citizens.

Workers continued to strike and U.S. businesses began to close their operations. By January 11, Lescot was asked to resign and he agreed to leave in May. The military placed him under house-arrest.

In May, the new regime held elections for congress and the presidency. Dumarsais Estime, a black moderate, was elected president and installed a mostly black cabinet. The mulatto elite had lost power, but massive blood-shed had been avoided.

During their farewell, Bettie and Francois had agreed to have no contact. He worried that receiving mail from the United States might mark him for attack by rebels, and they both knew they had no future together in either America or Haiti.

Bettie bounced around a series of odd jobs in Miami Beach. One of her jobs was as an audience plant in a comedy show. She pretended to be Miss Tennessee. This tiny taste of attention reminded her of how much she loved acting.

Why not move to New York and give a thespian career a try?

It was a mere suggestion. I doubt she even knew that *thespian* means "inspired by the Gods," but Bettie seized upon it. She had no friends or ties to Florida, and she had been able to save most of her income from her job in Haiti. Feeling adventurous, she packed her bag and moved to the Big Apple.

#

In New York, the acting opportunities weren't panning out, but she was able to get another secretarial job and rent a room in a boarding house. She worked for American Bread Company. Bettie had trouble making friends since everyone who worked at the Bread Company was older or married. Gone were the days of after-work drinks and dancing. Most of her colleagues raced to their cars to try and beat the traffic as they commuted to the suburbs.

She passed most evenings going to the movies. We started to get perturbed by how many of them were about murderous, cheating women.

"This is probably how Billy thinks of me," she thought as she watched Lana Turner in *The Postman Always Rings Twice*.

To counter her negative thoughts, I encouraged her to dream of stardom. As we watched *Humoresque*, I remembered how the stylist had tried to turn her into Joan Crawford during her screen test.

Just think, that could be you, staring opposite John Garfield. He's gorgeous. Imagine that's you, getting to kiss him like that.

Bettie enjoyed walking down Broadway after work, window shopping and looking at the advertisements for shows.

What will it be like to be a star?

"My picture will be on magazine covers and the world will know my name. Even after I die, people will remember my work. I will need to do something original, maybe even controversial, so that I stand out from the pack. Something like Jane Russell in *Outlaw*, or Rita Hayworth in *Gilda*," she imagined.

When not at the movies, Bettie spent evenings in her room reading. A benefit of the war was that her brothers had brought home books that were banned by the censors in America. Jimmie had given her Henry Miller's *Tropic of Cancer*, and she had devoured it in two nights. Jack had smuggled her a copy of *Lady Chatterley's Lover* by D.H. Lawrence.

Bettie flushed with heat and arousal as she read. "'Let me see you!' He dropped his shirt and stood still, looking toward her. The sun through the low window sent a beam that lit up his thighs and slim belly, and the erect phallus rising darkish and hot-looking from the little cloud of vivid gold-red hair."

I have to admit, aside from the racy novels, I was getting pretty board.

It's time you got out and socialized. Even Constance in the book realizes that she cannot live in her mind alone. A woman must be alive physically too. Don't you miss the sex? Now you know the variety of kisses and bodies and skills that are out there. How can you keep to yourself night after night?

I hate to admit it, but my libidinous urgings might have been the cause of what happened next.

#

The next evening, as Bettie was walking home, a good-looking guy in his twenties approached her. "Hey Doll, I'll bet with legs like that you gotta to be a dancer," he said and held out his hand. "The name's Chuck."

Bettie blushed and introduced herself. "I am not a dancer per se, but I do love to jitterbug." She smoothed her hair and noticed what an inviting smile Chuck had, along with his flirty little wink.

"My pals and I are going dancing," he gestured towards his Buick. Bettie saw another young man and a girl sitting in the front seat. They waved towards her. "I don't want to be the third wheel, ya know what I mean? How about joining us?"

"Sure," she said, happy to make some new friends in the city. They walked to the car, and Bettie got into the back seat with Chuck. She chatted with the girl in the front seat about shopping.

They drove a few blocks and, at a red light, two more guys jumped into the backseat. Chuck introduced them and they all talked about how exciting it was at the club they were headed towards. Farther on, two more guys jumped in the car, forcing Bettie to crawl up on Chuck's lap. He rested one hand on her thigh and curved the other around her waist. Everyone seemed friendly and chipper, but I sensed the sexual undercurrent.

I put her on alert.

Look, we are going over the Queensborough Bridge. What kind of dance clubs are out this way?

"Hey," Bettie said, "Where are we heading?" The men in the car exchanged glances and the guy sitting next to Chuck put his hand on her knee.

"We are going to a private club in Queens." He squeezed her knee and started to walk his fingers up towards her panties.

Bettie pushed his hand off, and said to Chuck, "I want to go home. I'm not comfortable with this." Chuck leered at her and winked. She called out to the driver, but he ignored her and continued until they reached a high school. The lights were out and the place was deserted.

The driver parked the car, and he and his girlfriend ran behind the gym. Chuck grabbed Bettie's wrist with a hand that felt like a shackle. He opened the door and ordered her to get out. "We are going to have our own little party under the bleachers." Dragging her by her arm, he headed towards the wooden seats.

The four other men in the car tromped along behind them. One of them slapped Bettie's butt and said, "You look like the kind of girl who spent a lot of time under the bleachers in high school—am I right?" The other men laughed and made rutting noises.

Bettie's fear had turned her to stone like one of Medusa's victims. She meekly let herself be yanked towards the bleachers.

Wake up, try and get away! Kick them, bite—do something.

I shouted, but her mind seemed filled with cement and nothing could get through.

Bettie stumbled and that seemed to shake her awake. She tried to tug her arm free, but his grip was a vice. She kicked, but her soft loafers did no damage and just made the men laugh.

"Oh, we got a wildcat here," Max said.

If this had been happening to me in my goddess form, then I could have used my powers to escape. I remembered when Artemis was about to get raped, she turned her assailant into a stag. His own hunting hounds then chased him down and tore him to shreds. While inhabiting Bettie, I could feel sensations through her body and speak in her head, but I wasn't able to physically make her move or run.

I wished Athena were here. She would never have let Bettie get into this kind of trouble, and she would have had a strategy to get her out of it. Strategy!

Tell them you are on your period.

It was a long shot, but I knew some men were squeamish about that sort of thing.

"I'm on my period," shouted Bettie, yanking on her arm as the bleachers grew closer. Her shoes dragged over the dirt.

"On the rag? Gross," said Chuck and hesitated. The men exchanged looks with each other.

Chuck twisted his hand in her long black hair and forced her to kneel. "There are other holes that you can use," he said.

"Come on, I don't care about a little blood. Help me hold her down," said one of the men. He fell onto Bettie and started to pull up her dress. She fought and clawed and screamed. The man couldn't hold her still enough to unbuckle his belt, and his friends seemed reluctant to help.

"Man, she's being too loud. Just sick your dick in her mouth and shut her up," one of them urged.

Two men grabbed her arms and held them flat while her perpetrator got off of her. "Make her sit up," he said as he dropped his pants. They pulled Bettie up into kneeling position with her arms twisted behind her.

Chuck forced her face up with a yank of her hair and grabbed Bettie's jaw with his other hand. "If you bite his cock, I will fucking break your neck. Understand?"

Bettie nodded as tears streamed down her face. There was nothing we could do. Five men in a circle around her with her arms behind her back, and her hair pulled so hard she could feel it getting yanked out with each thrust.

I didn't use my powers, exactly, but I was able to pull Bettie away mentally so that she hoovered in a kind of out-of-body experience. All five men forced her to give them blow jobs. They made crude jokes about the ultimate circle jerk and bonded with each other. It made me sick. I have seen this scene in battle fields and back alleys across the globe, throughout the ages. Men.

When they finished, Chuck pushed her face forward into the dirt. He stepped on her back and pushed his hand against her head. "Every Saturday. This is what we are going to do—right, Doll?" He added his full weight to her back and yanked her head up by her hair. "Right?"

"Yes," sobbed Bettie. With a final shove, Chuck and his friends left. Bettie curled into a ball, sobbing and shaking.

You are going to be okay. I promise.

I thought of how I had used my own twisted birth to become a woman of power and influence.

What is my twisted birth story? Cronos, Zeus's wonderful father, overthrew his own dad Uranus. It was a brutal fight and, in the end, Cronos chopped his father's penis off with his sickle. Everywhere Uranus's golden blood landed, new organisms appeared. Blood on the rocks turned into winged demons called Furies, and blood on fertile soil turned into nymphs and satyrs. And the penis? Cronos threw it into the ocean. Sperm came out of it and made foam. The foam mixed with the sea and created Me. Horrible. I know! It isn't a story I'm proud of, but that's how I was created.

I was lovely from birth and the changeable seas taught me graceful movements and how to have beauty in all situations. I learned how to glitter like sunset upon the water, disrupt like an ocean storm, and overwhelm like a tsunami. I learned how to please, like a splash of cool water on a hot face, and I learned how make men dizzy and helpless like a whirlpool.

When I finally came ashore on the island of Cyprus, wherever my foot touched, tender grass grew and flowers bloomed, blessed by my presence. Whoever looks upon me sees their ideal woman. Men project their own ideals and longings upon me. None of the men or gods who desired me actually got to know the real Aphrodite. I am a projection, and I'm okay with that. When others shame me and blame me for things my beauty and charisma cause, I don't accept it.

They are blaming the illusion of me that they created for themselves. I know my truth.

I know how to gain true power through the joy of laughter and a wicked smile. I flirt, and taunt, and seduce to achieve my goals.

Bettie already had the raw gifts, but I was going to take her trauma and turn it into real power. Those men wouldn't shame her into obedience and submission. With my guidance, Bettie would be reborn.

I knew, with my help, Bettie could get through this. But first, she needed to go home and lick her wounds. She needed to heal before she could grow strong.

I coached her into standing, and we walked down to the street and flagged down a car driven by an old couple.

"Oh, my goodness," said the older woman as she and her husband helped Bettie get into the car. "Should we take you to the hospital?"

Bettie shook her head.

"You don't want to go to the police, do you?" The old man asked as he began to drive. From his tone, Bettie knew that she didn't.

I was disgusted by how little had changed since 1600 B.C. During that time period, a rape victim would be punished as an adulteress because she had, however involuntarily, defiled the property of her husband. In fact, the word rape means "to steal." Rape is about women being controlled by men and has always been considered a natural expression of male dominance. Men consider it their right because they can get away with it. Bettie's assailants would never be punished. If she went to the police, she would be punished through shame and blame. She had gotten into that car voluntarily. Through a man's eyes, and the police were men, she had asked for it.

A cold resoluteness settled over her. She brushed her tears away.

She took off her shoe and pulled out the worn $20 bill she kept in it for emergencies. It was a trick her Momma had taught her early on. "You never want to be stuck without money. Don't rely on the kindness of strangers," she had lectured Bettie and her sisters back in high school.

"Just take me to the nearest bus station, please," Bettie said. She clasped the comb the older woman sympathetically handed her and fixed her hair. She took the offered tissue and wiped the dust off of her face. "I'm going home to Nashville."

9

There's No Place Like Home

Bettie decided on the bus ride that she wouldn't tell a soul about her rape. She didn't know if she would receive sympathy or condemnation so she kept it to herself.

She went to Momma's house when she arrived in town. Her mother gave her a luke-warm reception.

"I don't know what you're doing back at my house. You have a husband and you should be with him." Momma said as she led her back to the room she had shared with her sisters. It had become a junk room filled with old magazines and clothes.

"I left him. You know that." Bettie grabbed stacks of the magazines and started to leave to toss them in the trashcan.

"Stop! I might want to read those magazines. Just leave them alone." Her momma pointed to the pile and waited for Bettie to put them back.

"Well, there's no room in here." Bettie had her hands on her hips and looked around. She figured her mother's life of hardship had made her afraid to throw anything away.

Her mother ignored the observation. "You crept away like a thief in the night. I gave Jack hell for helping you do that."

"I don't understand how you can judge me. You divorced Papa."

"After I tried and tried for many years to make it work. The man cheated on me, got that young girl pregnant. How could I stay after he had shamed me like that?"

Bettie pursed her lips and said nothing.

"What did that handsome Billy ever do to you? He was moody after the war, but that's to be expected. A good wife would have loved him though his pain instead of abandoning him."

"I tried, Momma. He was so jealous and angry. I could hardly move without making him mad." Bettie's voice cracked in frustration.

"What did you think marriage would be like? Sunshine and rainbows? Dancing and driving around in fancy cars? Marriage is work." Her mother shook her head and tapped on Bettie's framed graduation photo that hung on the wall. "And since when did you become afraid of hard work?"

Bettie sighed. "I don't know. Maybe you're right."

No! She is not right. Don't go back to Billy. See if your Daddy and Lulu will take you in.

Bettie picked up her suitcase. "I'll go over to Billy's now. But I can't promise he will give me another chance."

"That boy adored you. He'll be happy to take you back. Just be obedient and tone down your flirtatiousness. No man likes that in his woman."

Bettie nodded without a word and began the long walk to the better part of town. She rehearsed her apology speech on the way. I tried to talk her out of it, but she pushed me down and wouldn't listen.

#

Mrs. Neal answered the door. "Oh," she said in surprise.

"Who is it Ma?" Billy called from the living room.

"You'd best come and see for yourself," she said and left the door open. Bettie waited on the porch chewing on her bottom lip.

"Bettie?" Billy's hair, which had once been his pride, was greasy. He wore his high school football jersey, which made him look shrunken. His face bore at least two days-worth of stubble. He stared at her like a starving man.

Bettie took a deep breath. "I'm sorry I left you like that. It was unkind."

Billy rubbed his stubble. "Well, since you left, I've had a lot of time to think. Maybe I could have been a better husband––taken you out, tried to make you smile."

Bettie gave him a tentative smile. "I'm willing to try again, if you could find it in your heart to take me back?"

"Where have you been? I was too embarrassed to ask your Momma, but no one has seen hide nor hair of you for ages."

"I went to Florida." Bettie did not think she had anything to gain by letting Billy know she had been to Haiti. He had a racist streak, and she figured he would accuse her of sleeping with black men. "Then I went to New York but..."

"But what? Don't tell me you were trying to be a Broadway actress?" Her acting had become one of Billy's sore points. He felt it was fine for a student to act, but he had been angry to hear about her screen test in Hollywood.

"No, of course not," Bettie made a dismissing motion with her arm and gave Billy her sweetest smile. "I had a good secretarial job, but I got so lonely in the big city." She reached out and put her hand on his arm, noticing with surprise how he had lost the muscular tone that she had found so sexy. "I kept thinking maybe we could try again." She leaned forward for a kiss.

Billy pulled her into a crushing hug. I could feel his lonely desperate energy pouring off of him. It felt like a whirlpool sucking us down.

Bettie, please don't do this. You won't be able to escape again.

Bettie ignored me and tilted her chin up to kiss Billy's hungry lips. When the kiss broke, she whispered, "I'm going to be good wife to you."

Billy was so grateful to have her back that his parents took her in. She wasn't surprised by the coldness in their demeanor and felt that she deserved it.

I knew the reconciliation couldn't last long. Billy's broken neediness was repellent to me, and I suspected it was to Bettie too, even though she wouldn't discuss him. I kept quiet and let Bettie feel safe and lick her wounds. If she needed to do a few more turns on the Billy merry-go-round, then that was up to her.

She got a secretarial job working for the L&N Railroad and attempted to settle into life as a respectable married woman. She tried to be content with domestic life and staying at home with Billy. However, it didn't take long for her to get restless. Even Odysseus, after spending twenty years trying to get back to Ithaca, nearly went insane from the monotony and security of home. Only adventure makes a bold soul feel alive.

After their sweet reunion sex, Billy's jealousy began to rear its head. They went for nightly walks after dinner. Billy held her hand tightly. It felt like he was curbing his dog instead of strolling with his love.

One night, Bettie saw a boy she had gone to school with. She smiled at him and gave a little wave. He crossed the street to chat with her.

The classmate had married a girl Bettie knew from debate and the pair had recently had their first child.

Billy silently fumed during the conversation. Embarrassed, Bettie tried to wrap it up. "Great to see you. Congratulations on your new baby, and say hi to Pam for me."

Once they were in private, Billy turned on her with fire in his eyes.

"You slept with him, didn't you?"

"Him? No, of course not. He was dating Pam all through school."

"It's not like that would stop a slut like you."

"Slut? Don't you remember you took my virginity on our wedding night? How on earth can you accuse me of that?"

"After our wedding, then. Once I shipped out. You were catting around with him then. I saw it between you two, the passion."

Bettie sighed. "You saw passion between me and him? You're imagining things."

"I know that look in your eyes. You either had sex or want to have sex with him."

"I only have eyes for you. We have sex every day, it isn't like you don't keep me satisfied."

"Sometimes I get so embarrassed that I married you. I see the look of pity in everyone's eyes when they look at me. They wonder how I could have been duped by a whore like you."

Billy was right. He did see pity in everyone's eyes. He just didn't know the cause. It pained the town to see their golden-boy football star reduced to a shell of the man he had once been. It hurt them to see all that potential wasted.

"I lived with your parents while you were gone. How could I have been sleeping around?"

But logic and argument could not sway Billy from his certainty that she had slept with all the men in town. Going out together became a trial. Bettie avoided saying hi to old friends and would try and lead Billy down uncrowded streets. Any encounter with a male became a source of accusations and elaborate stories that Billy would spin about her infidelity.

Billy reminded me Argus, Hera's favorite watchman, and Bettie was poor Io.

One day, Hera spied a cloud hoovering over a place where it didn't belong. She was immediately suspicious and descended to Earth. Zeus heard her coming and changed his lover, Io, into a snow-white calf. Hera pretended to be fooled and pet the cow tenderly.

"Oh, dear husband, please give me this beautiful calf as a gift," she said, batting her own cow-eyes at him.

Zeus couldn't deny his queen the gift without admitting his trickery. Hera took Io to her garden and tied her to an apple tree. She ordered Argus, her faithful servant to stand watch. Argus was the perfect guard because he had a hundred eyes all over his body and never closed more than fifty of them to sleep. Poor Io was forced to eat grass and live chained to a tree with no affection from Zeus or any mortal. Month after month, Io mooed her sadness to Mount Olympus, and finally Zeus felt pity on her and ordered Hermes to save her.

Hermes came to the garden disguised as a troubadour. Argus, bored from watching a cow, was happy to invite him in. First Hermes played a peaceful, sleepy tune on his lyre. Argus closed fifty eyes to take a nap. Hermes then began a story. It was the dullest story ever told with no beginning or end, wandering side-bars, and cliched dialogue. As the story unfolded, Argus closed his remaining eyes one by one. Hermes then placed a spell on him so that Argus fell into an eternal sleep. He had been bored to death.

Hermes untied Io, and she bolted out of the garden. It didn't take long for Hera to discover the treachery. She mourned for her lost Argus. She turned him into a peacock so that his one-hundred eyes would be immortalized on its famous tail. She then sent the vicious gadfly to chase and harass cows wherever they roamed.

Poor Bettie, there was no Hermes to trick Argus into falling asleep. There was just Billy, watching her with his one-hundred eyes.

#

I never predicted the straw that would finally break Bettie's back. The evening started typically enough, with the pair sitting in the living room. Mr. and Mrs. Neal had gone out to the movies. Bettie sat on the couch beside Billy, reading Raymond Chandler's latest novel.

Billy stared into space, occasionally grimacing. I suspected he was living inside his memories of the war. I have seen this happen to warriors throughout the centuries. The only thing that changes is the name of the malady——nostalgia, shell-shock, battle fatigue, irritable heart, war neurosis, or combat stress reaction. Every generation makes up a new name for the physical symptoms, depression, and memories that replay like a loop inside their soldiers' minds——a horrible gift from Ares to mankind.

"How come you always have your nose in a book?" Billy demanded, startling Bettie.

She took a deep breath and showed him the cover of the book. "It's just a detective story, you know, like on the radio show *The Adventures of Philip Marlow*."

"Why not just listen to the show? Why do you need to read the book?" His tone was aggressive and accusing, as though the topic were something far more controversial than reading.

"I don't know. I guess the story is better and more detailed in a book. To turn it into a script, they have to leave a lot out. You should read it. I'll bet you'll love it."

"Reading is for girls or college kids."

"I wouldn't say that. President Truman never went to college, but people say he's the best-read president of modern times. History is his favorite subject."

"So, I guess you think you're going to be president? Ha. You got that fancy college degree, but you are only a secretary, just like every other uneducated woman in town."

Bettie shook her head, She reminded herself to be patient with his nonsense. "No, I wouldn't even want to be president. Can you imagine making the decision to drop the atomic bomb? How could you live with yourself?"

"He had to do it to end the war. Damn Japs would never have surrendered. They were so strong, so unbreakable." A tortured look passed over his face. Billy ripped the book from her hand and threw it against the wall. It landed face down, splayed open, with the pages folded.

Bettie jumped up and rushed over to the book.

"Darn you, it's a library book." She picked it up, smoothed the pages flat, gently closed the cover, and rubbed the dent from the top of the spine.

"You touch that book with kinder hands than you ever touch me."

Bettie felt humiliated that Billy would speak about their sex life like that after she was trying her hardest to act passionate and compliant. Before she could help herself, she snapped, "It provides me with better entertainment and far more satisfaction." The second the words left her mouth, she wished she could suck them back.

Billy stood up and walked towards her. At 6 feet 2 inches, he towered over Bettie. "You think you are better than me. You think you are so smart with all your reading. You always have." She could feel the anger radiating off of him in waves. Bettie looked down, and cowered like a beaten dog.

Stand up. Don't let him intimidate you. Think of how those men in New York treated you. This man is your husband, but he still expects you to crumble and crawl before him. Do not shrink and submit before a man ever again.

Miraculously, my words struck a chord within Bettie. She stood up to her full 5 feet, 5 inches and looked Billy straight in his eyes. "This marriage isn't going to work. I tried my hardest. I wanted to be a good wife. But you won't let me dance, you won't let me have friends, and now you won't let me read. I'm only twenty-four-years-old, but you want me to act like I'm eighty. How can I stay if you won't let me live?"

Billy sputtered, but her words struck a chord of truth within him. He didn't try and stop her as she left the room, packed her suitcase, and walked out the front door.

#

She moved into the YWCA in Nashville and filed papers for divorce, ending her four-year marriage.

Billy didn't take the news well. The day he was served papers, he cornered her outside of the Y. Startled by the desperation in his eyes, she listened instead of running away like I urged her. Billy was her weakness. She was miserable with him, but felt guilty for cheating on him while he fought a war that had stolen his spirit and damaged him beyond repair.

She also hated the thought of failing at marriage, just like her parents. The media pushed the idea that marriage was bliss, and domesticity was the goal for women. I, along with her true nature, were fighting a constant battle against societal conventions.

"Baby, you can't really mean to go through with this?" Billy pleaded.

"I don't want to, but I can't stand your rages. The jealousy. The accusations. Everything I do, anyone I talk to, makes you crazy." She shook her head and tried to back up from him, but she was against a wall. "I can't live like this."

Billy grabbed her hand and held it against his heart. "I know. I know." His eyes looked so sad, her resolve weakened. I groaned. Billy continued, "I've tried to change, but it's all your fault."

"My fault?" The pity Bettie had been feeling left her, replaced by hot outrage.

Billy tried to caress her hair, but Bettie leaned away. "You make a man want to kiss you

—— that smile, that glint in your eye. You know exactly what you are doing."

"I am just being myself," she said. It was sort of true—Bettie was a natural. She had the lithe movement of a cat and the joy she radiated made men want to possess her. However, Bettie, even without my help, knew exactly how attractive men found her, and she used it as a subtle weapon.

"Sir, step away from the lady." It was the doorman at the YWCA. Some of the girls had seen the encounter and rushed to get help. He tapped Billy on the shoulder with his bobby stick. "Did you hear me?"

Billy dropped his hands and stepped back from Bettie. She quickly slid behind the security guard. "She's my wife," he growled, but his fight had left him.

"Well, it sounds like she's not going to be for long. Run along Buddy, and let the girl go."

Billy stared at Bettie and his eyes were filled with lust, anger, and regret.

Bettie felt sympathy which I chased away.

Let him go! Free yourself from him. He will never change. Fly away from this man, from this life. There is so much more waiting for you.

"This marriage is done," she said and turned her back on Billy.

10

Bohemian Life

Bettie headed back to New York to give her acting career another chance. She needed to do more than dream about success. This time, I wanted her to pursue her goals with passion.

Do everything as if it were the last thing you were doing in your life, and stop being aimless, stop letting your emotions override what your mind tells you. Focus on your acting goals.

I may have borrowed heavily from Marcus Aurelius in my motivational speeches——no need to reinvent the wheel every millennium.

Bettie moved into a studio apartment in Greenwich Village. To pay the bills, she took a secretarial job for real estate developer with an office in the Eastern Airlines building of Rockefeller Plaza.

To pursue her true career, she joined a group theater. Due to her thick Southern accent, she wasn't given many parts. Bettie spent most of her time as a theater apprentice and did scene painting and props and stage management.

As a reward for her service, she was finally given a bit part. She was cast to play Mable, a floozy in the comedy *Three Men on a Horse.*

"Of course, they gave me the floozy role. Is that the way everyone sees me?" She grumbled.

No one looks at a beautiful woman and wonders if they are smart. You're sexy and perfect for the role. You can't let the smallness of the part get you down. It can be an advantage to be underestimated. That gives you a better chance of wowing them.

It didn't take long for my advice to come to fruition.

The play was a comedy about a man with an almost supernatural power to predict the winner of horse races. He bumbles into the company of some shady gamblers who use him for his gifts.

Bettie only had a few lines, but she performed them with exaggerated expressions and excellent comedic timing. Her natural grace and fitness made the physical antics of the slapstick comedy easy. Her talent showed early on in rehearsals. Typically, her success attracted jealousy.

"I just feel that Bettie is overacting," complained Anne, the woman playing Patsy, the female lead. She was sitting in the audience, watching Max, the naïve hero of the play, react to the overt sexuality of Mabel.

"What are you talking about?" Phil, the director, responded. "It's a farce, she's doing great."

Anne pouted. "I just feel like she is upstaging Max, and he's supposed to be the star."

Bettie stood on the stage listening to their exchange. "I saw the movie version, back in '36. I'm trying to play the role the same way."

Anne put her finger in the air like she had a Eureka moment. "Exactly. Instead of putting an original spin on the role, you are a copycat. In this theater troupe, we strive for originality. You are an unimaginative doer."

Zeus save us from the Bohemians. Spoiled rich kids, they had such high ideals about how life should be lived. Those who didn't live up to their ideals, like those who worked in the existing world, received their cynicism.

Just ignore her. You are doing great.

Instead, Bettie ignored me. She continued to try and earn Anne's approval. Bettie couldn't see the trap she had fallen into. She tried the role different ways and, the more she strived for perfection, the more she lost her natural charm.

"Maybe you ought to take a break," called the director. "Fool around with the part at home. It's just a minor part, and we have a lot of ground to cover in rehearsal today."

You know that Anne is sleeping with the director. Now he is on her side. You will never be perfect or win over a jealous woman. Be yourself, that is where your power lies.

Bettie heard me as she left the stage. I hoped she'd find the original joy with which she had first performed the role.

Feeling like a failure, she went backstage to find Joe, the stage manager and ask for her next non-acting task. Joe had a theater degree from an eastern university, and he lorded his expertise over the theater apprentices.

"Bett, you didn't paint that backdrop the way I asked," said Joe.

"I just changed the shade of red a little to make it more vibrant. I thought it would be fun to make it look like the boardgame that went with this play."

"There was a *Three Men on a Horse* boardgame?" Joe hid his surprise with a disdainful tone.

"It was super cute. You had little wooden horses that could hold three flat wooden men. The first player to get around the racetrack with all their men won." Bettie remembered that it been one of the two games that the orphanage owned, and she and her sister had played every day during their hour of recess. Like the movie star posing game, it was one of her few happy memories of that time.

"How quaint," Joe said. "How about you follow my artistic vision, instead of copying the game." He put the can of red paint into her hand. "Such a waste, now you have to do it over."

#

Bettie arrived at her apartment to find a letter from Billy. Apparently, her mother had given him her address. The letter was long and apologetic. Billy reminded her of their happy times before the war and promised to be a better husband if she would just give him another try.

I could feel her emotions sliding into that special pit of nostalgia and guilt.

He threatened you when you got the divorce. Remember that. Don't even think of forgiving him.

"He sounds genuinely sorry and so sad. Maybe I should give him the benefit of the doubt."

I knew this was her loneliness and frustration talking. From experience, I know that the best way to get over a man is to get under another man. I decided to keep my eyes open for Bettie.

The theater is a world unto itself and a newcomer has to navigate it carefully. Bettie tried hard to fit in with the cast and make new friends. However, her Southern upbringing made it difficult for her to find common ground with the Northeastern WASP culture that the actors had grown up in.

In the evening, around ten of them would gather in the director's apartment, listen to Charlie Parker records, and talk politics. Bettie arrived one evening to find the party well underway.

"Suburbia is a prison. We seek spiritual destinies, rather than chasing the material things," announced Max, the great looking blonde that played the leading man.

He patted the cushion beside him, and Bettie joined him. She looked hip and sexy in her black leggings, black turtleneck, and beret. She had kicked off her flats by the door and her pretty little toes were painted red.

Stoke the fire of his attraction. He's gorgeous and sleeping with him will get him on your side. Then you will have leverage against Anne. Max might even get you better parts.

Bettie snuggled a little closer under Max's arm. She still didn't drink so she let the flask the actors were passing around pass by her.

"Hey, Bettie, you want some tea?" asked Marion, a girl who was obviously in love with Max, and not happy with the new competition.

"Sure," Bettie said. She shook her head in confusion when Marion passed her a joint. Everyone laughed.

"Man, you are one square cat," Marion said.

And she is a horny alley cat jealous of you and the attention you are getting. Ignore her.

Bettie grabbed the joint from Marion and took a long drag. The smoke burned her throat and set her into a fit of coughing. Everyone laughed. Bettie jumped up and ran to the kitchen to drink some water from the tap.

"I'm such a nerd," she said to herself. "I don't even want to go back in there."

Drugs and drinking are easy. You have sex appeal, something most girls don't. Why don't you get Marion's goat and give Max a kiss?

Bettie returned to her spot, and snuggled Max until her put his arm around her. She turned towards him with half-lidded eyes.

"I'm not that square," she whispered and gave him a lingering peck. When he responded with a French kiss, Bettie put her hand on his chin and imitated her favorite movie kissing scenes. She knew everyone in the room was watching them, and she loved it. An actor whistled appreciation. She made the kiss go on and on, pulling his head back towards her when he started to pull back.

When they finally finished, Max stared at her with dazed eyes. "Wow" was all he could say.

It didn't take long for Bettie and Max to become lovers, but he didn't step up and defend her from Anne's snarky comments or make any effort to advocate for her.

Fortunately, Bettie found her way back to herself and performed her Mable role with zany perfection. The laughter of the audience sent a thrill through her heart.

After the play closed, the acting group decided to stage a serious drama. There was one female lead. Bettie practiced the lines in private and surprised Max with a mini-audition.

"What do you think?" She asked.

"You did a fine job," he replied. Bettie felt a prickle of annoyance at his haughty tone.

"Will you talk to the director? Put a good word in for me?" She tried to keep the desperation out of her voice, but she knew that without Max's recommendation, Anne would automatically get the part.

"I don't feel comfortable doing that." He quoted Walt Whitman, "To have great poets, there must be great audiences."

"So, you just want me as your audience?" Bettie asked.

"You exist as you are and that is enough," he answered. Bettie rolled her eyes. As an English major, she recognized the poetic references and wasn't as impressed with Max as he was with himself.

You will find success on our own path. You have something special. It is better not to rely on a man for fame, or reduce yourself to the part of an inspirational muse.

Bettie continued dating Max, but the friction between them increased. Working as a stage apprentice for stuck-up Joe lost all pleasure. She found it harder and harder to bite her tongue at the nonsense her acting friends spouted and their privileged ennui.

One morning, Bettie turned off the alarm and started to get ready for work. "Life is meant to be celebrated. Anyone or anything—like religion or a job—that tries to drag you down and tell you not to have fun is wrong," said Max, as he tried to pull her back into bed.

"You want to know what really drags you down? Poverty. Guys like you, born with silver spoons, don't get it. There is no Daddy at home paying my bills," she said as she dressed in her modest work blouse and skirt.

"I'll be your Daddy," he said. Naked, he got out of the bed and wrapped his arms around her waist. She wriggled out of his grasp like a cat that didn't want to be held.

She turned to him with a serious expression. "You don't get it. Poverty isn't an abstract idea. It's a cage, and you'll do anything to get out of it." She touched up her lipstick and put it into her purse. "I'm never going to depend on anyone. I need my independence."

She turned and started to march out. At the doorway she paused, "I'm sick of your judgement. I pay for this apartment so I think it is time for you to leave."

"Come on, don't be like that."

"I'm going to take a break from acting and from you," she said. She stood with her arms folded and waited for Max to get dressed and leave.

He tried to give her a kiss as he passed, and she turned her head away. She closed the door after him with a hearty slam.

Good for you. When you close one door, a window opens.

#

Later that week, she was riding the elevator up to the office on the ninth floor and noticed a gorgeous Latino staring at her with a grin. She smiled back.

"I'm Carlos," he said, extending his hand. "I am looking for the Peruvian Embassy." Bettie loved his accented voice and the way his p's sounded like a little purr.

"Oh, I'll take you. I work right next door," she smoothed her hair.

"I've never been to Peru, but I knew a guy in Haiti who told me that Machu Picchu is incredible."

Carlos looked pleased at her interest and told her about his country. The conversation flowed easily, and she learned that he was a student from Lima, studying engineering at New York University. He was dealing with immigration issues at the embassy.

"Could I have your number?" He asked. Bettie felt her heart skip at the passionate look in his long-lashed brown eyes.

Bettie fished a paper out of her purse and wrote down her phone number. By the time she got home, the tenants on her floor told her phone had been ringing throughout the day.

#

Carlos and Bettie dated exclusively. She was never happier than when they were in bed, caressing his firm muscles and running her fingers through his curly chest hair.

Entranced by her Tennessee accent, something he hadn't heard before, he closed his eyes and ask her to repeat *talked, saying, isn't* and *you all*."

"Tawked, sayin', ain't and ya'll," she said and pantomimed a country girl.

Carlos was an incredible lover, even better than Francois, whom Bettie had thought was the pinnacle. Carlos loved to perform cunnilingus. He would kiss her until she felt drunk with desire and then smile as he slowly kissed his way lower. Bettie's legs would spread of their own accord, anticipating his attention. Between her legs, he would stop and inhale deeply.

"My breath of life," he would whisper. He would gaze at her pussy, with a look of reverence on his face, and she felt like the most desirable woman in the world.

Bettie had been taught by society to be worried about her scents and odors, but Carlos made her proud to be a woman. He released her from any shame she had been culturally conditioned to feel. His tongue would French kiss her pussy and, no matter how many times he ate her, he could always find new tricks to increase her arousal even higher. She would cum over and over, until she was begging for his kiss on her mouth so she could taste herself on his lips.

When he entered her, they would stare into each other's eyes as the exquisite sensation of that first moment of entrance overcame them. Carlos could make love with her without climaxing, bringing her to orgasm over and over, before finally finding his own release.

She called him her favorite drug and wondered if this was the kind of pleasure that the heroin addicts on the street were feeling. She could see how chasing these sensations could become an obsession.

However, when they weren't in the wonderland of their bed, they faced challenges as an interracial couple.

"Everyone thinks I'm a Puerto Rican," he grumbled and gestured towards a sign hanging in a window, "No dogs or Puerto Ricans. And you Americans sure aren't welcoming to them."

"I'm sorry," Bettie said, caressing his arm.

"Spic lover," shouted a man, standing in the doorway of a bar.

Bettie tightened her grip on Carlos when he made a move to confront the heckler. "Don't bother with him. You know the police would love to toss you in jail. You can't win so just ignore it."

He stopped on the corner and looked into her eyes. "Why doesn't it bother you? They are insulting you too."

Bettie put her hands on his chest. "I don't care what people think about me." Carlos rolled his eyes, so she explained. "There is no point in worrying what people think because you don't have any control over it. When I was a little girl, my Momma was always accusing me of running around and doing things with boys, even though I was still a virgin." She sighed. "Nothing I said could ever convince her. Then, after I got married, my husband was the same way." She started to walk again, as if trying to outrun the past.

"Hang on, *querida*," Carlos called as he caught up with her. He kissed her full on the mouth, no longer caring about the judgements.

Bettie kissed him back, her lips transmitting her fearless passion to him. "I'm just myself, and I let other people be themselves. I mind my own business."

They started walking along the street again. "Is that why you are so happy all the time?"

"Probably," she reached up and caressed his cheek. "It is amazing how much power you have when you don't care what other people say, think, or do."

#

Carlos shared Bettie's passion for dancing. The pair would go to Spanish Harlem and the South Bronx to take in the live Latin music. Carlos taught her how to mambo and samba, but it was the rhumba that Bettie loved best.

She bought Xavier Cugat's albums, and the two of them would practice on the kitchen linoleum.

"The cha-cha and rhumba are two stages in a woman's life. The cha-cha is the dance of flirtation," explained Carlos, "It is faster with a light-hearted feeling." He put on a cha-cha song and demonstrated. "One-two-three cha-cha-cha. Be sharp with your turns and movements, make your skirt swish."

He and Bettie danced through a song. She was careful to follow his tips while keeping a flirtatious smile on her face.

"But the rhumba," said Carlos, taking the needle off the record, "is the dance of two lovers that have found each other. It is the dance of seduction. The slow dance made to build desire, a dance of foreplay."

He put on a rhumba song. "One and two are quick steps and get one beat of music each, but hold three and four for two beats of music. Use those slow steps to build sexual tension." Carlos demonstrated the steps himself, and Bettie felt the heat of arousal.

She danced, channeling her inner vixen on the slow steps. She looked at Carlos with half-lidded eyes and gave him a hint of a smile and bit her bottom lip. Carlos whistled. Bettie adopted her Southern Belle pose with a fan-like hand. "I've been told by some gentlemen that I'm kinda sexy."

Carlos growled and pounced on her. They laughed as they fell onto the bed.

#

Carlos surprised Bettie with tickets to *Streetcar Named Desire* on Broadway. "Look at the playwright's name, it's Tennessee Williams. I figured you would love to see a play by an author from your state."

"He is actually from Mississippi, not Tennessee, but I'm thrilled to go. The reviews say his work is a perfect example of Southern Gothic," said Bettie. "A bunch of my friends in the Village have seen it, and they loved it."

I was thrilled too. Hermes had been inhabiting Tennessee Williams since his college days. Hermes is the God of Travelers and anything related to the road, good and bad. His greatest gift is wit and a magic with words. He coaxed Williams into writing about forbidden topics, like homosexuality, and inappropriate desires. Through his plays, Williams created conversations about the unmentionable.

Bettie gasped when Marlon Brando walked onto the stage. He reminded her so much of Billy. She remembered his blue-collar roughness. How much she had loved to see him use his hands to fix things then use them on her body with that same matter-of-fact manner. She had forgotten how that stirred the cave girl in her. She glanced at Carlos. He was a true Latin lover, slow and romantic and attentive. Like Francois, and her Village friends, he had the smooth, uncalloused hands of an intellectual. There was something so primitive and virile about men like Brando and Billy.

I knew the attraction, after all I'd spent centuries on and off again with Ares. However, I felt a shiver of dread realizing her thoughts were going down that well-worn path. How could she watch this play and pine for Billy? The brutishness of Brando should have eclipsed his sex appeal.

When the play was over, the pair walked down Bleecker Street toward the Village. Carlos glanced over at Bettie's closed face. "You're awfully quiet. What did you think?"

She cleared her throat. "It kind of disturbed me. That rape and the way everyone just pretended it never happened."

Carlos shrugged. "What good would it have done anyone to call the police? Stella had a baby so she didn't want to be alone and poor."

"I know. It was realistic." Bettie sighed. Carlos reached for her hand, but she felt agitated and crossed her arms across her chest. "It was also Blanche Dubois, her fragileness. It reminded me of my Momma. She liked to bend reality too. She was always hoping the next man was going to do right by her, even though he never did. It's strange, she always told me never to rely on the kindness of strangers."

"But that's what Blanche does the entire time. It's practically the closing line of the play," said Carlos.

"And look what happened to her. I guess the kindness of strangers must be a Southern thing, something she heard her Momma say growing up." Bettie shook her head, frustrated by her unwanted memories. "My Daddy was so bad. His affairs—it was a constant humiliation for her. But even after she divorced him, she picked boyfriend after creepy boyfriend. She only ever had one quality man, but he was a strict Catholic. To get him, she pretended she had never been married or had kids."

Carlos looked stunned. "That's a pretty big lie."

"No kidding. Of course, he found out. It's pretty hard to hide six kids, especially when she didn't even let us in on the trick. My brother Jack accidently blew her cover when he went home, after getting discharged from the army, and asked to see his mother."

"Did they get divorced?"

"Yes." They waited at the corner for the light to change. "I never met him, but I always felt bad thinking that Momma forced a staunch Catholic to get a divorce." She looked at Carlos, "But, you can't build a relationship on lies, so he had no choice."

Carlos cleared his throat. "Do you wish you hadn't seen the play?"

"I don't know what to think," she said. They heard a band playing from a bar up ahead. Bettie grabbed Carlos' hand and tugged him towards it. "I do know that dancing always gets my mind off my troubles."

#

Their affair continued, and Bettie often spent the night in his apartment. She laughed when she thought of how she'd grown up judging people who lived in sin.

"I'm loving my sinning," she whispered as Carlos took on his seductive devil persona, put her onto the kitchen counter, lifted her skirt, and started to pull off her panties. She heard a banging on the door and looked over.

"Carlos, open the door! I know you're in there with her!" They heard an accented female voice from the hallway.

Bettie knew at once who it was from the look on his face. "Don't tell me you're married?" She hopped off the counter and started gathering her things.

"*Querida*, it isn't what it looks like. She was in Lima, and I was here." He gestured weakly and straightened his own clothes. The pounding continued.

"Open the door," Bettie commanded.

With a look of fear, Carlos obeyed. The woman flew at him in a rage. Tearing at his hair and pounding on his chest. Bettie watched and felt shame fill her. She had seen a picture of the woman holding a young boy in his wallet. When Bettie questioned him, he had assured her it was his sister and nephew.

I knew at the time that it had to be his wife. Afterall, a man doesn't carry a picture of his sister in his wallet. However, Bettie wasn't suspicious so I didn't alert her. I don't have a problem with having affairs with married men, after all, what's good for the goose is good for the gander. The only thing I worry about is a Hera wife, but I had figured that Carlos was safe in the U.S. I was obviously wrong.

"Puta! Whore! Home wrecker!" The brunette shouted, as she spied Bettie over Carlos's shoulder.

Bettie felt like a snake. "I'm sorry, I didn't know," she whispered and pushed past the woman into the hall. She half expected the woman to turn and attack her, but she saved her rage for Carlos, and the two of them shouted at each other in Spanish.

Days later, Carlos showed up at Bettie's door with roses and an apology. Nothing he said could convince her to stay.

"You have a son!" She flashed back to her own parents' battles and felt horrible knowing that she was doing that to another child. Carlos cried and tried to kiss her. She relented and gave him a long good-bye kiss. Holding each other close, they both wept and expressed their love.

"I'll never forget you," Bettie said, "but we can't build a relationship on lies." With a sad smile, she closed the door on him.

#

Goldie was getting married, so Bettie took the bus down to Nashville to be her matron of honor. What is it about a wedding that makes even the most independent woman lose her mind? The red and white roses, the band playing romantic ballads, and the bubbling champagne are tributes placed upon the Alter of Marriage.

Bettie danced and flirted with guests at the wedding, but her mind ran through arguments about why she needed to give her marriage another try.

You have already tried twice with Billy. Do not even think of going back.

"Maybe third time's a charm," said Bettie.

Your feelings are hurt. You need time to heal from Carlos. Don't to go backwards.

"When I was a little girl, the thing I wanted more than anything in the world was to not be a failure like my parents."

You aren't a failure. What are you talking about?

"I failed at my marriage. I failed at Max and Carlos."

You moved on from bad men. You escaped relationships that had problems. Those men were more to blame than you for the ending.

"I look at those relationships and the common denominator is me. Clearly, I'm the failure."

I wish I could say that Bettie's way of thinking was unusual. Unfortunately, women always want to blame themselves. We have been so ingrained with the need to be nice and loved and accepted. Most of us feel that our worth comes from other people.

Please don't go back to Billy. Give yourself grace. You are still so young and have a life of new loves and experiences ahead of you.

But her resolve was strong. Billy was her link to the past. The totem she always turned to when her world fell apart. Once she got back to the City, she called him up and invited him to stay with her in New York. He jumped on the next bus north.

At first, things were great. Billy was filled with remorse and apologies. "I know I've been a bad husband, but I promise to change."

He got a job for a local cab company and the pair settled into a domestic routine. A boring domestic routine. Billy had no interest in visiting the coffee shops to see Beat poets. Gone were the nights spent dancing or visiting the theater. Billy hated the sound of jazz and complained constantly about the noise of the City.

Bettie wondered why she had romanticized Billy's lovemaking while watching Marlon Brando. His made sex feel like a demand, not a request. He went so fast that she never came close to reaching climax. She longed for the smooth hands and endless foreplay of Carlos.

"Let's go back to Nashville," he said after one of their sex sessions. Bettie had hoped he would fall asleep, like he usually did. She was so tired of this argument. "We can buy a house. I'll even go to a specialist to see if we can find some help getting you pregnant."

Billy had been told by a doctor that the mumps he had as a child might have made him infertile. The volatility of their marriage, and the memory of her own childhood, made Bettie count it as a blessing.

"I don't care about having a baby. I've told you that," she said. "I want more than just keeping house down in Tennessee. I like my life up here."

"Well, I hate it," he said and threw his beer bottle against the wall. Bettie didn't flinch, instead, she rolled her eyes. His macho dramatics had become a cliché.

I knew what needed to happen. I counseled her.

End things with Billy. You think he is a safety net, but he is a curse. Having this escape route keeps you from fully committing to your career. Sometimes you have to run your ships aground, burn them, and leave yourself with one option--succeed or fail. You will never get what you want as long as you leave a ship on the beach.

Bettie still waffled. "I feel so bad about my behavior during the war. I was having fun while poor Billy was being destroyed."

It wasn't a trade. The war would have destroyed him even if you had sat home every night. You shouldn't feel guilty. You didn't have any control over what he experienced. You keep trying to make this marriage work, but you it won't because you are both different people now. The war trans-formed Billy into someone angry and suspicious. San Francisco, Haiti, Francois and Carlos have transformed you into someone bold and adven-turous.

Billy had switched from anger to pleading, and this was how he always got her back. He stumbled through apologies and tears as he cleaned up the broken beer bottle. I tried a different tactic. If Bettie wanted to feel guilty, I'd let her.

Look how pathetic he is. He isn't the man you fell in love with when he is like this. You have reduced him to a weakling. Stop teasing him. Do you really want him? Let him go. Release your hold over him, and let him live like a man.

That got to her. "Stand up," she demanded. Billy complied with a surprised look on his face. "I need to be fair to you. I don't want this marriage. I was just scared to be alone." She put her hand on his shoulder. "Go find a woman who wants what you want—the house and the kids." Like a sorcerer she gave him a final kiss, and said, "I free you. I won't call you again."

I summoned my son Eros and asked him to remove the arrow of love from Billy, so he would leave without a fuss. Bettie's constant pulling him in and pushing him away was getting tedious. It wasn't fair to Billy.

11

The Discovery

Once Billy left, Bettie had a new spring in her step. On a beautiful fall day, she visited Coney Island. She strolled with the crowds on the boardwalk, dressed in her jeans with rolled cuffs, and a tight, white sweater.

"You pays yous money and yous take your choice," shouted the ride hawkers. Bettie loved all the spinning and clanking––wild rides like the Cyclones roller coaster, the clown shoe spinning cars, and the Tilt-a-Whirl.

Bettie joined a flirtatious boy for a trip on the Ferris Wheel, but ditched him when it was over. She wasn't ready for a relationship. Alone, she rode the parachute drop three times in a row. She felt like she was in a blossoming petunia as she looked up at the pink and white striped parachutes that started closed like a bud, and then spread open as the swing dropped.

I was especially interested in the girlie shows. I love to see how different cultures entice their men. The hawker caught my attention, "Ladies and Gentlemen. We have the fastest stepping girls in the business. Shake dances, exotic dances, and the Dance of Temptation."

Let's check out the dancing.

"It will be kind of weird to go in there alone—as a girl."

Since when do you care what people think?

She stood outside the hall and watched the show girls dressed in their belly dance costumes, holding out their sheer fabric skirts, and parading in front of the entrance.

The hawker noticed Bettie. "This show is for ladies as well as gentlemen. But don't think you are going to a Sunday school picnic." His eyes admired her figure but he sneered at her childish Bobby socks and loafers. "Don't you go in, sit in the front row and then, after the show begins, run out here crying, 'You shocked my modesty.' Cuz I ain't given you your money back."

Bettie paid him the twenty cents, more to stop his tirade than anything else. The hall was dark and filled mainly with men. Bettie squeezed into a bench next to the aisle, the man next to her kept his leg pressed against hers. She clenched her knees together and made herself as small as possible. The hall darkened and the show began.

The so-called "dancing" was limited to girls walking around in skimpy costumes. They would look vacantly at the audience and twist this way and that. A flash of leg from behind a curtain brought howls from the easily entertained young men. The belly dance was a joke. Back in Ancient Greece, the dancers were rhythmic and sensual. They knew how to shimmy and do a proper figure-eight hip role. Most importantly, harem girls knew how to flirt, tease and entice with their eyes and smiles.

These girls look uncomfortable and checked out. Definitely unsexy.

"They look like they aren't having any fun. I wonder why they do it? They could just as easily be a secretary like me," thought Bettie.

Bettie scooted out of the show before it ended because she didn't want the man next to her to try and follow. The sun was setting and the crowds had thinned. It was the doldrum time when the sun worshippers and families left, but the night-time groups of men and couples on a date had yet to arrive.

Bettie walked down the wooden boardwalk towards an area usually populated with body builders. Bettie was a member of a gymnasium and, along with swimming, used the facility to lift weights. She enjoyed a well-toned male body as much as I did. The area was empty except for a handsome black man lifting barbells. Bettie sat down on a bench to watch.

The man preened for her, and the two exchanged glances. I was happy to see she was moving past her broken heart. When the weightlifter finished his set, he put his shirt on and walked up to Bettie.

"Name's Jerry Tibbs," he said, offering his hand.

Bettie introduced herself and the pair made small talk about weight lifting.

"You have a great figure. You ever done any photographic modeling?" He asked.

"I did a few ads when I lived back in San Francisco during the War. You know, the type in the newspaper circulars where the woman looks enraptured by her clean windows or new vacuum cleaner." She clowned around, acting out her delight.

"My hobby is photography. If you let me shoot you, I'll give you copies of the photos free of charge—you can make a portfolio and shop for other modeling jobs with it."

He looked honest, but I cautioned Bettie.

This might be a trick to lure you into a place alone and molest you.

Bettie recalled the horror of the night in Queens when she had naively trusted a man to take her dancing. She made her excuses and started to leave.

"Hang on," Jerry said and pulled a card out of his wallet. "I know this sounds shady, but you can trust me. I'm a cop––New York City's Finest."

As Bettie studied the card, a lovely white woman with brunette hair walked up and laid her arm on Jerry's. "Is my husband asking you to model?" She asked.

"Why, yes, he is." She looked between the two of them. The woman had a beautiful figure with large breasts and a tiny waist.

"I told him he scares the girls when he does that. Listen, he's a good guy. I can stay in the room during the photo session if it makes you feel more comfortable." She looked up at Jerry with eyes of love. "No way this lunk will mess around on me—right?" The pair laughed.

Bettie loved their easy camaraderie and felt at ease. She agreed to go meet the couple at their apartment the next day.

#

In his apartment, Tibbs had a backdrop set up in the living room. Large circular reflectors leaned against the wall and the atmosphere was professional.

His wife brought out a box of bikinis and helped Bettie figure out ones that would fit. She stuffed Kleenex in the tops to make Bettie fill them out better. Jerry directed her on how to pose in popular pin-up styles and suggested different facial expressions.

The photos were terrific and Jerry was able to sell them to a Harlem newsprint magazine. He and his wife had Bettie over for dinner and presented her with five different issues where she appeared on the cover.

"I had no idea!" Bettie said, as she marveled at the magazines. "You are a really good photographer," she said.

Jerry smiled but answered, "You are a great model—a natural. You look so happy and relaxed. Every man's dream of the girl next door."

His wife cleared her throat. "Listen, are you okay with the magazines? Harlem is a black neighborhood. I told Jerry to run the idea by you before he sold the photos, but he said you wouldn't mind."

"Are you kidding? I don't mind at all," she answered.

"I'm happy to hear that, but surprised. Jerry and I get so much abuse when people see us together. We can't even go to a restaurant. We mostly have to stay at home to keep white men from picking fights with him." Her voice started to crack. "I love Jerry with all my heart, but society hates to see a white woman with a black man. I don't know if you understand the kind of bad publicity this might bring you."

Bettie spread her hands out on the table and looked at both of them. "When I was a little girl, growing up in Tennessee, I hardly knew any black people but everyone told me they were bad. Then, one day I was walking down the street flipping through my baseball cards and two black girls came out and started picking on me. They knocked the cards out of my hand and ran away with them, so I figured it was true that black people were bad."

Confused by the story, Jerry and his wife looked at each other then at Bettie.

"But then I moved to Haiti and mostly everyone there was black or mulatto. I made so many dear friends. I realized then that people are people—white, black, Latino—we're are all the same. Good ones and bad ones." She shrugged her shoulders and gave the Tibbs a beaming smile.

"I guess it's because you've left the U.S. You have a bigger perspective than most," said Jerry.

"Travel cures all prejudices," said Bettie, echoing what Francois had told her.

#

Bettie continued to model for Jerry Tibbs. The more photos he took of her, the more obsessed he became with making her look perfect. He reminded me of Pygmalion.

An introverted sculptor, Pygmalion had sworn off real women. Instead, he spent his days carving ivory, always seeking to create an ideal female. He would nearly finish, then discover an asymmetrical ear or an imperfect fingernail and, in a frenzy, smash the statue and begin again. I knew his perfectionism was coming from sexual frustration and realized the only solution would be for him to get laid.

At last, after endless attempts, he created the perfect statue of the woman of his dreams. He made generous offerings of myrtle leaves, roses, and swan-meat at my temple and prayed to me.

"Please give me a bride that is the living likeness of my ivory girl."

He had been a devout and generous worshiper, so I decided to grant him his wish. When he returned to his home, he kissed the statue.

"Her lips feel warm," he said in wonderment.

He kissed her again, running his hands along the marble which slowly came to life and soon began kissing and caressing him back. I had transformed the ivory into Galatea.

They were married at once. I'd like to say they lived happily ever after, but there is a reason stories always climax at the magical first kiss and close with the marriage ceremony.

Pygmalion soon became bored with Galatea, a real woman with wants and needs of her own. It didn't take long for him to return to his studio and carving—this time he focused on creating the perfect dog. A companion that didn't talk was more his style.

Tibbs, similar to Pygmalion, spent most his time in his studio. "There is something wrong," he said, studying images spread out on the table. He had tried post-photo improvements like retouching her face and painting on longer eyelashes. He looked from the photographs to Bettie, back and forth. "I know what it is," he said, slamming his hand down on the table. "It's your protruding forehead."

"What?" Bettie asked, trying not to have her feelings hurt by his assessment.

"Fluff your hair foreword," he directed, "eliminate your middle hair part."

Bettie did as she was told. When she flipped her head up, she left her hair covering her face. "Tada!" She said from behind the hair. "An improvement, I'm sure."

Jerry folded the front hair over, making it look like bangs. He turned Bettie towards the mirror on the wall. "See, bangs will make your forehead look smaller."

Bettie studied her reflection. She could see that he was right. Until then, she had always worn her hair long and parted in the middle, often held back by a head band.

"Give me some scissors, and I'll do it," she said. Jerry found a pair and followed her into the bathroom to coach her on how to cut them. They looked at her reflection in the mirror. Bettie reached for a tube of red lipstick, and applied it.

"Perfect," they said in unison.

I 2

Camera Clubs

As Tibbs's images of Bettie appeared on more and more Harlem magazines, it didn't take long for his Camera Club buddies to start asking him about the new girl. He asked Bettie if she would be willing to pose for other photographers.

"I'm always happy to work, but what are Camera Clubs?" She asked.

"I've got this friend, Cass Carr. He runs the Lens Art Camera Club and a couple of others. He hires models and then charges photographers a fee to take pictures of the girls." Tibbs paused and watched Bettie's face as he added, "they usually want nude poses."

Bettie bit her lip as she thought about the last part. "Is it pornography?"

"Technically no. There won't be any sex, simulated or real. It is just girls in the pictures, and you don't have to do anything you are uncomfortable with." Tibbs started to pace the room.

Bettie watched him, curious over his anxiety when she felt none. "The nudity doesn't bother me. I've even thought about joining a nudist colony. I just don't want to do anything illegal." Her father had spent a year in prison and she heard enough stories from him to know she didn't want that to happen.

"The photos are for private enjoyment." He made a jerking off motion with his hand. "They won't be published anywhere. It becomes pornography if it gets mailed so it gets tricky trying to sell nude photos to magazines."

"Mailed? That's what makes something pornographic?"

Tibbs faced her and rubbed the back of his neck. "It's crazy. Some law made back in the 1800s says it is illegal for the US mail to send or receive works containing obscene, filthy or––" he paused and made quotation marks with his fingers, "inappropriate material."

"Inappropriate must cover a lot," said Bettie.

"All information about sex, even birth control," Tibbs shrugged. "That's the last great barrier to free love, the fear of pregnancy."

Bettie had heard from her Village friends that scientists were working on a pill to prevent pregnancy. She'd believe it when she saw it. "I don't think the moralists will ever allow that to happen. God-forbid a woman be allowed to control her own body."

"I need to be upfront with you," Tibbs continued. "The guys in the Camera Clubs––some are real photographers, like me, but a lot are just voyeurs. I don't even think they all have film in their camera. A bunch of nerdy squares anxious to see a sexy girl in real life," he stopped his pacing and met her eyes. "Are you okay with that?"

Voyeurs, how fun!

Voyeurs were the perfect match for exhibitionists like me and Bettie. She didn't know that trait about herself, but I did. Tibbs was tying himself in knots, unable to imagine that a woman could feel comfortable with perverts looking at pictures of her. He couldn't fathom the power that gave a woman. Bettie would be safe. She would be the girl at a distance, flirting, teasing and taunting with no risk of harm. What could be more fun than that?

Hephaestus, my nerdy, introverted husband, also couldn't imagine the power of Exhibitionism. He thought he could shame and humiliate me. He learned about my affair with Ares from that old busy-body Helios, who spied us as he drove the sun across the sky. Using his metallurgic skills, Hephaestus crafted a golden hunting net, with mesh so fine it was invisible. He positioned it above our marital bed and announced that he was leaving to visit his family under the sea. As soon as he was gone, Ares and I tumbled into bed. Let me say, Ares likes things rough, and when the bed shook as he pounded me, the net fell and ensnared us in *flagrante delicto*.

Suddenly, Hephaestus appeared. He tried to look outraged, but I could see his arousal. He was a cuckhold at heart. He dragged the net containing Ares and me up to Mt. Olympus where all the gods gathered around and laughed at us and jeered. I feigned embarrassment, but I loved it. I loved the idea that Hephaestus had seen me with a real lover who knew how to please me, loved that all those male gods in Olympus saw me doing with Ares what they all wanted to do themselves, and loved the horror and judgement on the goddess's faces. They wished they were half as desirable as me.

Ares, of course, became furious. He was so sensitive to any criticism from his father, Zeus. Hephaestus demanded that our marriage be annulled. Zeus couldn't agree to that. He had given me to lame-o Hephaestus to prevent the other gods from fighting over me. Besides, Ares was an affair; those didn't matter. After all, every male god on Mt. Olympus had affairs. This was just shocking because I was a goddess and neither monogamous or chaste.

As punishment, Zeus forced Ares to pay Hephaestus his marriage price. It was nothing of consequence. What value did money have for immortal gods? In the end, Hephaestus was left with less than he had started.

Now I could openly carry on with Ares, and we publicly acknowledged our daughter, Harmonia, a lovely girl who symbolized peace through the union of love with passion. We also had two sons, Phobus and Deimus, that I'm not as proud of. They became Ares's right-hand men and rode into war inducing panic and fear. I threw Hephaestus a bone and pretended that Eros was his son, but the God of Love was really the offspring of Ares too.

I knew Bettie would feel just like I had in that golden net. She loved to be the center of attention and adored for her perfect body—it only seemed fair to share it with others.

#

Bettie agreed to meet with Camera Club organizer, Cass Carr. He was a black Jamaican, musician, bandleader, and photographer who ran the Lens Art Camera Club in Harlem and the Concorde Camera Circle in Midtown.

Carr was a wolf, filled with energy and purpose. He would book up to ten photographers for a shoot. At first, Bettie posed in his studio. She put on the sexy look and the pursed lips of Hollywood sex kittens. She even tried to look like a Greek goddess, with arms upraised and eyes cast down. The photos were good, but not magical.

Carr quizzed her about why her photos with Tibbs had been so much better.

"I don't know. He and his wife became my friends, so it was a homey atmosphere. But I think it's more that I don't like your studio."

"Why is that?" He looked around the dark studio, not seeing the peeling paint, smelling the musty odor of old fabric, or feeling the coldness of the equipment and steel folding chairs.

Bettie knew better than to insult him so she said, "I just don't feel inspired. Every shot is always in front of the same backdrop, that orangish one with the patterns."

"Okay, Miss Fancy Pants, how about shooting outdoors? Would that please you?" Tibbs asked, anticipating her shock at the suggestion of posing nude outdoors.

"That's a terrific idea," she said. "I love the beach and sunshine. We could also accommodate more photographers." Bettie thought about that for a moment and then added, "But I want more money. Twenty-five dollars a day for outdoors, not the ten you pay me for inside."

"You better make it worth the extra money," Carr warned and studied Bettie. "Why don't you can all the pouty sex-kitten stuff. You aren't a blonde like Jayne Mansfield or Marilyn. Be different. Pretend to be the wholesome girlfriend these guys had in high school, but become the girl that actually puts out when you get her alone."

"I can work on that," said Bettie, her wheels already turning.

"Plan on this Saturday. I'll take you and a couple of girls out to Jones Beach. I know a little spot where we can have privacy."

"Great! I'll pack a picnic lunch," said Bettie and left with a skip in her step.

#

In the days before the shoot, I advised Bettie.

Most models come without vision or emotion. They have no craft. You are an actress, use your craft. The camera is a man. What kind of man is he? You decide before the shoot. Is he a shy man, yearning to be seduced? Is he an uptight businessman wanting to lose control and be led astray? Is he a fellow hedonist and the shoot is just foreplay before your hot sex? Are you a nymph playing in the woods, unaware of the mortal watching you?

"Oh, I love the idea that the camera is one man. If I think that way it is easier to ignore all the photographers crowding around me. I'll keep each photo session fresh by imagining different types of men looking at me."

Bettie brought craft to each and every shot. Soon photographers were calling Carr, asking in advance if Bettie was going to be present. Events with her had twenty-five men, and Carr would have to turn some away. They would form a semicircle around Bettie and photograph her simultaneously. Many of the photos showed the shadows of the shutterbugs, but no one seemed to care.

Bettie's favorite locations were at the beach.

"You looked like a little otter, splashing out there in the surf," said Artie Amsie, a sweet regular with a huge crush on her.

"I love the ocean and the sand. I have so much fun."

"And it shows." Artie gestured towards three models huddled under a blanket. "Look at them, freezing their little tushies off over there. And here you are, soaking wet. That water-must be sixty degrees, but no one would know to look at you."

Bettie liked Artie, but I reminded her to play the coquette––to give herself during the shoot, but pull back, and leave all the men wanting more. She treated each gig as though she were a model in an art school. She would laugh and charm the photographers, but, when the camera's stopped clicking, she made it clear that she was finished and unavailable for other activities or dates.

Carr wisely selected his locations. However, one time Bettie was modeling for a different Camera Club and the organizer picked a spot too close to the highway, near a small community in upstate New York.

A woman driving by on the road saw topless girls in bikini bottoms and called the police. Squad cars arrived with sirens blaring. Bettie barely had time to get dressed before she, and the other models and photographers, were trundled down to the local station. I coached Bettie.

This is art. The Camera Club is creating art using models like you. This is no different than the naked statues and paintings made during the Renaissance. If an officer harasses you, tell him you were recreating Sleeping Venus by the painter Titan.

Bettie tried my approach, but the cop snorted and said, "Art? Okay Venus, I'm going to charge you with indecent exposure.

"I'm not indecent," Bettie proclaimed.

With her urging, all of the models and photographers refused to plead guilty to any charges. The police tried to wear them down and kept them in the jail for five hours. But Bettie's obstinacy, and the fact that there was no clear definition of indecent exposure on the books, caused the police to dismiss them with the promise that they would return to the City.

"Where all the perverts and degenerates live," the officer added under his breath.

#

Inspired by my references of classic artwork, Bettie carried herself like a demi-goddess. She changed in private and wore a silk robe between shoots. The men were in awe of her and never took secret photos as she changed poses.

She came alive in front of the camera. She acted like a devilish child with a glint in her eye that showed she didn't take anything too seriously. She was brazen, blissfully uncaring, and light-hearted.

"The modern world is so manufactured and artificial. But not you, you are like a lightning storm, an eclipse, a sunset. You are nature personified," gushed Artie.

I worried that Artemis might take offence by that statement. We goddesses don't like to hear mortals elevated to our levels. I think it was just Bettie's poor judgement, and not Artemis, that orchestrated what happened next. But, I'll never be positive.

Normally, Bettie never drank or smoked. She hated the smell of cigarettes and the taste of alcohol. But mainly, she feared anything that might make her lose control. But, one night, after a shoot, she agreed to go to a house party with a group of photographers.

She didn't realize until she got there that the party consisted only of photographers and no women.

"We brought something special, just for you, blackberry brandy," said the organizer. Bettie initially said no, but the man encouraged her to just take a sip.

"It is so sweet. It tastes amazing," said Bettie. She gulped it down like it was soda pop and held her glass out for a refill. The men topped her glass off before she had even finished the second drink.

Be careful. Sweet drinks go down easy and you'll be drunk before you know it. Why don't you switch to water or milk for a few glasses?

She ignored all of my warnings and drank too much. I could see the barely hidden glee on the men's faces as they watched her get buzzed.

"You're looking beautiful tonight. Run your fingers through your hair and muss it up, like you just woke up," one of the men suggested.

"Can you give us a little strip tease?"

Bettie complied, languorously removing her dress and bra.

"Take it all off, Sugar."

She undid her garters, bent over, and rolled her stockings down her legs. With a flirtatious glance over her shoulder, she pulled off her black panties and kicked them to the side.

"Sit over there, on the couch," ordered another. The men gave him a warning look, "err, please." Bettie lounged like a feline on the couch, her eyes half-lidded as though she had just woken up.

"Beautiful, Doll, beautiful." Bettie heard the shutters snapping and smiled sleepily to herself. She could picture how beautiful she must look because she felt like she was floating on a cloud.

"Spread your legs a little more, that's right."

"Touch yourself, like you do when you are all alone."

Stop obeying them. Wake up.

Bettie felt sleepy and lazy. A man came over to the couch and ran his finger from her toes up to her hip. Her back arched in response. She felt another hand caress her arm and begin massaging her shoulder. A third hand delicately cupped her breasts.

Get out of here. You are going to get raped.

My warnings finally got through Bettie's head. Adrenaline

flooded her system and she was suddenly wide awake with a racing heart. She pushed herself off the couch and started to get dressed. She stumbled around the room, searching for her shoes.

"I need to go home," she pleaded.

The largest of the men offered to walk her home. The other guys whistled and made suggestive remarks as they exited. A few offered to accompany them, but were silenced with a glare.

Bettie staggered through the street, leaning heavily on the man. Interestingly, her drunkenness started to repel him. He wanted the confident Bettie. The middle-America soda pop girl with a naughty side. He didn't want a drunken slut. Once they arrived at her house, the man said good-bye at the door and left.

The next morning, Bettie shook off her hang-over with a strong swim and put cucumbers under her eyes to reduce the swelling. She barely remembered what had happened the night before.

13

Men's Magazines

Cass Carr filled Bettie's schedule. She had camera shoots indoors and outdoors, nude and in bikinis. I encouraged her to burn the last ship she had on the beach.

Commit to this life. Quit your secretarial job and fill your time modeling.

She took the plunge and enjoyed the perks of sleeping in and having the freedom of time and money.

She moved into a larger apartment. She repainted it, sewed curtains and slip covers in a yellow tropical print, and retiled the bathroom.

"It was seedy when I moved in, but I made it cute," she told Artie during a studio shoot. "I even bought an aquarium with angel fish and guppies. I call them my miniature friends."

"Sounds like you are making a cozy little nest," he said. He adjusted his stereo camera. "Alright, the camera is going to take two photographs simultaneously at different angles. Remember how I told you to pose."

"I remember," she said. She leaned forward so her breasts hung towards the camera. She was nude, although he had her hide her pubic hair in most images through her angle, or with a well-placed fan or flower bouquet.

"I wonder how different these 3-D photos will look."

"Good enough to eat," mumbled Artie.

She lifted a mirror and a brush and held the pose perfectly still. Then she dropped the props and lifted a beckoning finger towards the camera.

"Now go put on your black bra and panties, the one with the braided trim. Don't forget the fishnets."

"Oh Artie, you and your lingerie," laughed Bettie as she put them on.

#

A camera club photographer tried to sell some of his pictures to Robert Harrison, the leading publisher of the men's magazines *Wink, Titter, Beauty Parade* and *Eyeful*. Harrison saw potential in the raven-haired model—someone different from the blonde-bombshell type that dominated the modeling world. He gave her a call.

"I've got a specific formula for my mags so I need you to work with my photographers—are you game?"

Bettie was always happy to work, and the magazines paid better than Camera Club shots. Her theater background came in handy, as she filmed spoof scenes printed in a comic book style. In *Gal and a Gorilla,* she played a sweet girl, protected by her gorilla escort, a man in a hairy costume. She recreated the famous King Kong scene and befriended him. Bettie skated in a bikini while the gorilla followed on a scooter. She had him doing her laundry and taking her on picnics, all the while flashing her long legs and high heels.

With another model, she played a bikini-clad sailor. The two, just inducted into the Navy, clumsily swabbed the decks and did target practice on a silhouette with giant boobs.

"It's all so silly. I feel like a clown," she told Goldie over the phone.

"I see you on the covers too," Goldie gushed. "I loved that blue bikini you were wearing in *Bold*."

"Thanks! I've been sewing up a storm. I bring my own swimsuits to those shoots. They fit me better that way."

"You aren't always in a swimsuit. I saw those nude pictures of you on the beach in *Modern Sunbathing*."

"The publishers call themselves a 'health magazine' and that is how they can get around the censors and publish nudes. 'But the nudity has to be tasteful,' the editor told me." Bettie paused. "Where are you seeing those girlie magazines?"

"I found a stack in the back of Momma's closet," squealed Goldie.

"Are you kidding? I didn't know she knew what I was up to. I figured she would be ashamed."

"Well, she tells the neighbors that you are working as a secretary in New York, so she obviously isn't crazy about it. Still, she buys your magazines so she must be proud."

Bettie hoped her mother wouldn't find out about her other modeling gig. Momma wouldn't be very proud of the work she was doing with Irving Klaw.

#

Bettie was introduced to Irving Klaw and his sister Paula by a Camera Club photographer. The Klaws ran a magazine called *Movie Star News*, but had a profitable side-business selling fetish photos.

Irving invited Bettie to his studio and Paula, both a photographer and the designer of the shoots, showed Bettie the costume room.

Bettie walked slowly, touching the fancy silk and satin lingerie and expensive black leather gloves and handmade heels. "I've never seen heels this high," she said, examining a black boot. She pressed her finger against the stiletto heel.

"We have those made by an Italian bootmaker," explained Paula, "smell the leather."

Bettie took a whiff and it brought me back to the heyday of Rome. Italians have always had a gift for shoemaking and, throughout the ages, their leather has been the softest and best smelling.

Paula opened a chest. "These fetish enthusiasts have money. They bring in their own costumes." She pulled out a latex catsuit and passed it to Bettie.

She felt the stickiness of the latex and the petroleum smell. She crinkled her nose and handed it back to Paula. "I prefer the leather."

"Look at this chain outfit."

Bettie laughed and held the chain-mail up to herself. "Metal against soft skin. It is erotic." She shook it to hear the tinkles of the tiny links. It reminded me of the golden net that Ares and I had been trapped under. She pointed at a trunk spilling over with ropes. "Why do you have all of those?"

"Bondage. They're our best customers." Paula picked up a rope and dragged it over Bettie's skin so she could feel how silky it felt. She started to tie her wrists together. "There is a specific way to tie the ropes and position the models. I had John, my main contact, teach me all the intricate knots and techniques."

When she finished, she looked up and saw Bettie's worry. "Don't be afraid. It's all pretend. You won't actually be hurt, although we might tell you to look like you are in agony."

"I'm not so sure," said Bettie looking at her wrists lashed together with a complicated knot. When she pulled her hands apart, the knots grew tighter.

The silk ropes and intricate knots reminded me of how Odysseus had his men tie him to the mast of his ship while they sailed past the island of the Sirens, near Scylla and Charybdis. The Sirens were once the attendants of Persephone, but had been transformed into half bird-half- woman monsters as punishment for allowing her abduction by Hades.

With the bodies of birds and the ability to fly, the Sirens had the heads of beautiful women and arms with which they played the lyre. Their honey-sweet tones and songs would bewitch sailors who, in their quest to find the beautiful singing maidens, would break their ships upon the rocks. The Sirens would then feast upon their bodies like ravens and vultures.

Odysseus had plugged his crew's ears with wax to protect them, but he wanted to hear their seductive songs himself. He had directed his crew to tie him to the mast so that he wouldn't jump overboard and heed the lure of the Siren songs.

The bondage fetish echoed the desire to be unbearably aroused, yet unable to act upon it. Maybe the desire to see the woman tied up was a patriarchal twist on the myth—a desire to see the Siren tied and helpless instead of the man.

#

Paula freed Bettie from the ropes. "Come into the office and talk with Irving and me," Paula said, leading the way out of the costume room. Irving sat at his desk, looking at a proof-sheet with a jeweler scope. He stood up and shook Bettie's hand.

"I had Paula show you the costume room right away, so you know what you are in for if you decide to work with us."

"It seems so—" Bettie hesitated, not wanting to insult the photographers.

"Let me read something to you," said Irving, picking up a hardback. "This is an important book. I'll loan it to you, and it might make you understand things better. It's called *Sexual Behavior in the Human Male*. It's written by Kinsey, a scientist, and based on over 5,000 interviews with American men."

Bettie looked at the orange book with its bold title written in black capitals. "I had friends in the Village that talked about it, but no one ever had a copy they were willing to loan me."

Irving opened up the book and began to read. "Whatever his sexual background each person reaches the limit of things he can understand because of his own experience...Beyond that there are always things which seem esthetically repulsive, provokingly petty, foolish, unprofitable, senseless, unintelligent, dishonorable, contemptible or socially destructive." He glanced up at Bettie to see her reaction.

She knew her cheating on Billy was considered dishonorable. I reminded her of other things.

Your affairs with Carlos and Francois—society considered them contemptible and socially destructive. Yet, those men made you feel alive and beautiful and you caught a glimpse into different worlds by looking at things from their perspectives. Would you trade in those experiences to please a judgmental society?

"I think I am starting to understand what you are getting at," Bettie said.

Irving continued, "Gradually one learns to forego judgements on these things and accept them merely as facts."

"I look forward to reading the book," said Bettie reaching out her hands for it. I couldn't wait to dive into the research and see what it had to say about men. As much as I consider myself an expert, there are still many areas of their psyche that I don't understand.

"Come back when you've finished it," said Paula as she walked Bettie to the door. "I think Kinsey's discoveries, as well as our generous wages, might help convince you to model for us."

As soon as Bettie got home, she poured herself a glass of milk, put on the record, *Charlie Parker with Strings*, and dove into the book.

"From the dawn of human history, from the drawings left by primitive peoples, on through the developments of all civilizations, ancient, classic, Oriental, medieval and modern, men have left a record of their sexual activities and their thinking about sex…It is an interesting reflection of man's absorbing interest in sex, and his astounding ignorance of it; his desire to know and his unwillingness to face the facts." Bettie read.

I thought of how homosexuality was esteemed in ancient Greece yet reviled today, how men's feminine ideal had embraced both Rubenesque and waifish bodies, and how the quintessential man can encompass both the brutish warrior and the effeminate poet. I couldn't help but notice that rules and modes were determined by men. The patriarchal society model, found throughout the civilized world, always held the power.

"This is a report of what people do, not of what they should do, or what kinds of people do it…In our culture, sexual responses have been subject to religious evaluation, social taboo and formal legislation," read Bettie.

She got up, turned the record over, and refilled her glass, reading all the while. "50% of males have extramarital affairs, compared to 26% of females," she read. "I felt so guilty for cheating on Billy, mostly because society expects wives to be faithful, but not husbands."

She snorted in frustration. Bettie remembered how she had guarded her virginity and been taught to dream of marriage, yet had felt her greatest pleasures and joy in the arms of men that society deemed unacceptable for a white woman.

How do women get power in a patriarchy?

I asked, leading her towards the decision I desired.

"They seduce a powerful man, and bring him to his knees through his weakness for sex. Then they get what they want by manipulating him," answered Bettie.

True, but a woman can gain power by herself by flaunting the rules of society. Men made these rules that women should be virginal until married, obedient, monogamous and modest.

"I already violate most of those edicts. I'm divorced with lovers, openly sexy, and proud of my nudity. I'm independent of any man."

What is the reward for obeying the rules of a society that disempowers you? Men project their fantasies onto your image. Does it matter? Does it hurt you? It isn't real. How do their fetishes and fantasies harm you? Why not profit from it? Follow your gut. Does the modeling feel wrong to you?

Bettie was starting to come around. "Kinsey found that 22% of men feel erotic responses to sadomasochistic images, and Paula said they had money. I'm already posing nude for Camera Clubs. What difference would bondage make? It is just like acting."

Bettie reported to the Klaw studio the next day.

Paula maintained strict order on the set. Men paid for the costumes and photographs, but they were never allowed to see the models in real life. Paula tied the ropes and arranged the women for each scene. The Klaws photographed only women, never men, and they always wore lingerie or costumes. Bettie took turns playing both the Dominant and Submissive roles.

"You have a knack," Irving said to her. "When I put that ball-gag in your mouth, you use your eyebrow and wide eyes to show your terror. But in the next scene, you tie the model up to the X-frame with such an evil, calculating look."

"It's my acting classes," Bettie said, as she slapped the manacles closed on her wrist and ankles to get ready for the next sequence. "This isn't really any different than the silly comic strip shots I do for Harrison."

"Wait to you see the pony costume that just arrived for you," said Paula motioning Bettie to lay herself across the other model's lap for a spanking. "Full-length leather bodysuit with a fringe mane and tail."

"Is it for a cowgirl scene?" Bettie asked, between spanks and clicks of the camera.

"Yes, but I don't know why he specifically requested you to play the horsey. The outfit hides your lovely face behind a two-foot pony head."

14

Florida

While working for the Klaws, Bettie continued modeling for the pin-up magazines. Posing constantly, for variety of photographers, she often didn't know where her images would end up. She would be shopping and stumble across her photo on *Ellery Queen Mystery Magazine*. It was a regular bikini picture of her, but the magazine had photoshopped menacing dark figures into the background.

Calendars, postcards, matchbooks, and playing cards held her image. "If only I got paid every time I got printed," she grumbled to Goldie during their weekly phone call. "I only get paid for the modeling session. Those photographers can sell the photos to whomever they want for any price."

"What about the record albums?" Goldie asked.

"Same deal. I'm on the cover of *Ain't Misbehavin,'* by Fats Waller and the *Carmen* album. That makes me pretty famous but not rich."

"I don't know. I think it would be amazing to be famous," said Goldie who by then was living the suburban life with kids. "Every day here is the same old thing—making peanut butter sandwiches, driving the kids, and playing nice with those prissy women on the P.T.A. I know I'm supposed to be happy, but––"

"Sounds like you have the housewife's syndrome. I went to a party in the Village and there was a shrink there. He described it as a certain emotional malaise, bordering on depression that he is seeing in more and more of his female patients."

"That sounds like me all right." Goldie sighed. "It's pathetic the way I wait all day for Fred to come home with gossip. I feel like he's from this exciting world, and he's just paying us a visit."

"I'll be down to visit you soon," said Bettie. "We can paint Miami red and eliminate your doldrums."

"Knowing you, I think we will paint it with cheetah spots."

The girls laughed, and Bettie continued, "I thought I could get a solid two months of rest while visiting you, but photographers down there keep calling to set appointments. Pretty big names like Hannau, Caldwell, and Correa. I also have a female photographer, Bunny Yeager."

"A female? How could a woman possibly know how to operate a camera? Or be able to take a good picture of a naked woman?" Goldie mocked.

"Shocking, I know," laughed Bettie. "She's an unknown, but I love posing for Paula Irving, so I figure working with Bunny might be fun. You can come with me to my shoots. You'll see it's a lot of standing around waiting, followed by brief sessions of intense activity." Bettie twirled the curled phone cord around her finger as she spoke. "No matter how long the shoot has gone on, I always have to smile and look sparkly and fresh. Modeling isn't as glamorous as you think."

"I think hanging around with you is what the doctor ordered. I'll get Suzie to take the kids. Heaven knows she's always pawning hers off on me." Goldie's voice slipped into a conspirator's whisper. "She's having an affair with the tennis pro. Her lessons often go longer than scheduled."

These modern housewives reminded me of poor Persephone. Like her, they had lived a life of naïve innocence. Walking in the sunshine, attending college, and believing that the future held even more bliss. Their Demeter mothers encouraged their ignorance, keeping them shielded from the compromises of marriage and motherhood. Unlike Persephone, the girls had willingly followed their handsome Hades, certain that life as a wife, as queen of her own world, would provide satisfaction.

It didn't take long to realize that her husband was the king of their world, and he controlled the money and family decisions. They were treated to new refrigerators and three-bedroom houses, the modern equivalent of the jewels and rare minerals Hades presented Persephone in an attempt to win her over.

Like Hades, their husbands couldn't understand why their wives weren't happy. Why did they long for their past lives in the sunshine? Why couldn't they be satisfied with the dim light of the Underworld?

Powerless, they stayed and gorged on modern pomegranate seeds. Ladies' magazines, like *Redbook* and *Good Housekeeping*, told them their role was sacred. Like a Greek Chorus, the magazines tolled: "You have the duty of maintaining the home fire, supporting your husband, the hero of corporate America. Stay at home and try this new recipe. Stay at home and plan a weekend cocktail party to practice your hostess skills. Stay pretty and thin."

"Housewives are Goddess of the Hearth," they declared. But they weren't. Hestia is the Goddess of the Hearth, and she had pleaded with Zeus to allow her to remain single. Hestia wanted to remain her own woman and not be a victim of the decisions of men. She saw, first-hand, how Hera and Demeter suffered from marriage.

Hestia maintained the hearth in Mt. Olympus. It was a position of power because this is where arguing had to stop. "Come to the hearth and reconcile," urged Hestia. "Warm yourselves. Gather strength, and go on your own path." When Gods would try and sow discord, she would order them, "Leave the Hearth. Do not return until you are willing to listen and hear the needs of others."

Bettie's sister wasn't Hestia, no one listened to her. She was Persephone.

#

Bettie got her own cottage in Miami so that she wouldn't impose on Goldie's husband. She also wanted to be able to sleep in and not be bothered by Goldie's kids. Her independent lodgings came in handy once she met Armond Walterson.

She was walking along the boardwalk and saw a young man in a white pullover shirt and shorts staring out to sea. His broad shoulders, V-shaped build, and tight ass attracted Bettie immediately.

She walked up to him and asked if he would mind taking her picture. When he turned around, she realized he was young, only eighteen or nineteen. She hesitated.

Come on, have a little fun. You're on vacation.

When he saw Bettie, his eyes nearly popped out of his head like a cartoon character. "Umm, sure," he said and reached for the small camera.

"My name is Bettie, by the way."

"Armond, Armond Walterson," he said as he hid his face behind the camera.

Bettie smiled her most engaging smile and posed her body in ways she knew enticed.

The poor boy blushed and fumbled with the camera. Bettie laughed to herself, knowing all the pictures would be blurred. He took a few shots then handed the camera back to her. She could see his hand trembling with anxiety.

"Do you want to go for a swim?" Bettie asked.

"Um, sure," he said, while looking at the ground.

As they walked down to the water, two of the boy's friends spotted him and ran over to join him. They weren't shy and laughed and joked with Bettie. Armond never said a word, despite Bettie flashing him smiles and touching his arm as she spoke.

Sensing that activity might make him more comfortable, Bettie challenged him to a swimming race, which he handily won. Then the four of them had a splash battle.

They were sitting in the sand, warming up, when a car honked. Armond glanced up, "I gotta go."

"Where?" Bettie asked.

"Home. That's my mom honking."

Be bold, before he disappears.

Bettie followed him up the beach as he jogged towards the car. "Do you want to go out with me?" She asked.

He stopped and stared. "Me? I thought you liked my friends."

Bettie touched his forearm. "Nope, you were the one I had my eye on."

"Wow. Yes, of course I want to go out with you. You're so pretty." The horn honked again. He looked over at it and waved. "Meet me at La Playa restaurant. You know where it is?"

"I do! See you then."

Armond left, and Bettie hugged herself. "It feels so bold and naughty making the first move."

That evening, Bettie had more opportunities to feel powerful. Armond was so shy and in awe of Bettie that she had to be the aggressor to make anything happen. After dinner, they went for a walk on the boardwalk, and Bettie paused to look at the sunset. She backed up into Armond's torso and reached to pull his arms around her waist.

He sighed and nuzzled her ear with his nose. Bettie turned in his arms and leaned forward for a kiss. Armond kept his mouth closed and mashed his lips against hers.

She pulled back and ran her fingers through his hair. "You don't have much experience, do you?"

He blushed and tried to pull away. Bettie kept her arm around his waist and caressed his cheek to calm him. "That's okay. I'm a very good teacher." She touched his bottom lip with her thumb. "Just follow my lead. I do, you do." She started with a sensuous closed mouth kiss and then progressed to Frenching.

"Mm, you are a quick learner," she purred. She threaded her fingers through his hair, and he did the same to her. She kissed along his chin line, and he imitated. Bettie had to keep from laughing because making out like this was so sweet and fun.

Whenever she wasn't working, she was with Armond. Bettie took his virginity. She taught him how to be an excellent lover. She told him exactly what a woman liked and how to go slow and when to be rough. She taught him how to caress, how to kiss and how to compliment. Everything she had learned from Francois, Carlos and Billy was passed on to Armond.

He was so young that Bettie didn't think he would be anything more than a vacation fling, but Armond followed her around like a puppy dog always wanting to be pet. They had two passion-filled weeks, but then his mom asked to meet the girl he was spending so much time with. She told her son to bring Bettie home for dinner.

Bettie carried a bouquet of flowers and rang the doorbell. The door was opened by a pretty older woman, whose smile was replaced by a frown.

"Why, you must be at least ten years older than Armond," she exclaimed staring at Bettie. Armond stood behind his mother, his face tense.

Bettie smiled, but inside she crumbled under the woman's judgement. "He's eighteen and seems to like me." She looked over at Armond who was chewing on his bottom lip.

"You ought to be ashamed of yourself. Taking advantage of such a young man." His mother pointed to the street. "Leave him alone. I'd better not hear that you have still been seeing him."

Armond said nothing, so Bettie turned and walked away. She remembered how many of her friends had gotten married at eighteen and felt it was unfair that Armond's mother was so overprotective of him.

Don't feel bad. He's an adult and now you have given him the ultimate gift of knowing how to please a woman. He'll be grateful to you his entire life.

#

Luckily, Bettie was too busy to mope. It was almost a relief to be single again because photographers kept calling to schedule her. Her sister came with her to nearly all of her shoots. She didn't mind all the waiting, and Bettie was happy to have her companionship.

"Bunny's getting pretty impatient out there," said Goldie as she came into Bettie's dressing room. Bettie wore a silk leopard print bathrobe and was taking the curlers out of her hair.

"Seeing as she's only paying me five dollars for this shoot, I think she can hold her horses." Bettie applied her make-up and picked up her hair brush. Goldie sat on a stool and tried on the red lipstick.

Bunny peeked her head around the corner. "Are you almost—" she paused, watching Bettie brush her hair. "That robe drapes so nicely. Let's start the shoot wearing it."

Bettie nodded and walked out of the dressing room on her tippy toes. "Why are you walking like that?" Bunny asked.

Goldie laughed. "She always walks on her toes when she isn't in heels. The kids called her 'Tippy-toe Bettie' in school."

Used to the teasing, Bettie wasn't defensive. She stretched out her leg with a pointed toe. "Look how much more attractive my legs look when my toes are pointed." She demonstrated standing flat-footed and on her toes. "I'm not tall like most models. I need every inch I can get."

Bunny nodded in agreement and directed Bettie to get on the padded rectangular bench in front of the back drop. I have to admit that Bettie amazed even me. She used that robe to express her feline nature and looked ready to leap out of the image and pounce on the viewer. She progressed, without prompting, to fully nude with the robe a prop held out behind her.

"You don't even seem naked," said Bunny. "Your skin is so evenly tan, and you have no blemishes—it looks like it was airbrushed."

"I've always sunbathed nude, I hate the look of tan lines. I think they are distracting," said Bettie.

Bunny continued to photograph Bettie nude, directing her to use the bench as a prop. Bettie turned it on its end, embraced it, leaned on it as if it were a man—all the while maintaining a sexy pout and "come hither" look.

"How about you put on some of that lingerie you brought," suggested Bunny.

Bettie left the room and reappeared in a sheer white bra with black sequins sewn on each nipple point, echoing the pasties of a burlesque costume. The sheer white panties had black trim and a two-inch waistband of black lace. She completed it with black stockings, rolled at the top to stay on without a garter belt, and black patent leather heels.

"Gorgeous," said Bunny.

Bettie pointed towards a large circular ottoman. "I'll turn this on its side." She did and it reached her waistline. "Now it looks like a circus ball."

"We just need to get you a whip and some lions," said Goldie.

"That gives me an idea," said Bunny.

#

Bunny arranged for a photo shoot at Africa USA, a jungle-style petting zoo. The night before, Bettie finished sewing a leopard-skin one-piece that she designed for the shoot. She tried it on in front of the mirror, checking for the final fit. The legs were cut up to her waist, with the side made up of six small strips of fabric. The suit hung on only one shoulder, like a Tarzan top, and she had made a small triangular skirt of fabric to cover her crotch, while still show-casing her legs. Pleased with the look, she took it off and practiced some modeling poses in front of the mirror.

Scratch, scratch. Bettie turned towards the sound, wondering if it was the wind. She heard a rustle in the bushes and knew at once that someone was outside her window. She grabbed her robe and turned out the light. She crept to the window and saw the dark shape of a man outside, taking the last of the latches off the screen.

"I'll give you two seconds to get away from that window, or I'll blow your brains out," she shouted. The man dropped the screen and ran away.

Bettie called the police. It didn't take long before a night watch-man, who patrolled the boats down by the river, came running.

Bettie told him what had happened. "I'll put this screen back on. Don't worry, little lady, I'll sit on your porch all night and make sure he doesn't return."

Bettie thanked him, but found it impossible to sleep. Her body was filled with adrenaline and she spent the night pacing. At sunrise the next day, she telephoned Bunny and told her what had hap-pened.

"I look horrible. There are bags under my eyes, and my skin is pale. We need to reschedule the shoot," she said.

"Absolutely not. Be a professional. I'll be by at 7:00 a.m. to pick you up and take you out to Boca Raton. Don't be late," commanded Bunny.

The pair arrived at Africa USA. Bettie wore her leopard swim suit and sat miserably on a stump. "I look like I've been on a big drunk," complained Bettie. "You are going to have to touch up every photo."

"You leave me to worry about that," said Bunny. She added powder to Bettie's face. "Just channel Tarzan's Jane. Smile and frolic, like you always do." Now go climb up that tree and look down at me. Foliage makes a good back drop."

Bettie, always a professional, pulled her actress skills into duty. She climbed trees and playfully romped through the bushes. She speared a fake fish in a waterfall and posed with zebras, camels, and a chimp that wore baby shoes.

"These ostriches are a little scary," Bettie called between smiles. "They have yellow dinosaur eyes and a sharp beak that they want to poke my eyes out with." She screamed as one flapped its wings and darted forward to peck the seeds from her outstretched palms.

"Take a quick break and go over to the cheetah pen," called Bunny, as she put new film into her camera.

In the enclosure, two cheetahs were led over to Bettie. The trainer handed two chain leashes to her. "This is Moja and Mbili. Their names mean one and two in Swahili."

"Are they safe?" Bettie asked. The cats had glassy eyes and panted with open mouths.

"They were sick all night," the trainer said. "But they'll be fine."

Bettie felt her heart race as she took their leashes. "I hope they don't take it out on me."

"Just don't let go of their chains. Cheetahs run 75 miles an hour. I would have a hard time catching them."

The cheetahs were pretty out of it and passively laid down for most of the shoot. Bettie straddled Moja and gave a low growl to the camera.

"Perfect," said Bunny. "I know that shot's a keeper. Now take off your swim suit."

Bettie knelt naked in the grass between the two cheetahs and pet their ears. She squealed when one of them licked her side with its rough tongue.

"That's about as dangerous as these two get," called the trainer. He had never enjoyed his job as much as he did on this day. After twenty minutes, the cheetahs started closing their eyes. "I need to give these two a break. It is time for their nap."

"We have one more scene to shoot," said Bunny. "Put on your Jane swimsuit. We are going to shoot comic-book style."

"What is the storyline?" Bettie asked, as she got dressed and touched up her make-up.

"The Cannibal's Cauldron," said Bunny, as they left the enclosure and walked to another part of the park.

"I'm Martin, your cannibal," said a well-built black actor. He was dressed in a leopard toga with white stripes painted on his face. He had on a feather mane that framed his face and grass arm and leg bands.

"Those remind me of a vodou dance I saw in Haiti," said Bettie pointing at the grass bands. Martin asked about the story, and Bettie told it as Bunny shot their story sequence.

It began with Martin ambushing Bettie and tying her up to a tree. He threatened her with a log spear and then went to start his fire. In the next shot, fire extinguished, Betty sat in the cauldron, looking over her shoulder in faux-fear as Martin licked his lips in hunger.

"I'll bet you will be able to sell those to Harrison. Silly cheese-cake comics are his favorite," said Bettie at the end of the shoot.

#

Bettie extended her stay in Florida. She enjoyed the companion-ship of her sister because she didn't have many female friends back in New York. She also loved the warm weather and was in no hurry to return to rain and snow. She worked nonstop for a variety of pho-tographers, but Bunny booked her most of all.

One day, Goldie laid on Bettie's bed and watched her get dressed. "Are you going out to the beach again?"

"Yes, today it is Key Biscayne. Do you like this suit?" She modeled a red, Hawaiian print bikini. "See how I put a button here on the bottoms?"

"It's terrific. I'll bet you could be a swimsuit designer once you get too old to model," said Goldie.

"I am—I just don't make any money off of it," said Bettie.

"What do you mean?"

"This couple hired me to do a shoot at Jones Beach. They told me to bring every bikini I owned. When we got to the beach, they had me put on each bikini and would shoot only four photos––my front, back, and side while standing. Then the last photo would be a pin up pose. I should have been suspicious, but I was too trust-ing." Bettie shook her head and lifted the pile of swimsuits out of the drawer, letting them cascade back down. "They ended up taking all my swimsuits and calling them their own designs. They sell them in *Charmand's Catalogue of Fashion.* The kicker is that they use my pho-tos in the advertisements." Bettie shook her head.

"You can sue. Have you gotten a lawyer?"

"No, I don't have time for that. My days are booked with model-ing gigs. It's not like I took out a patent on my bikini designs. I don't think anything would stand up in court."

"You're probably right," said Goldie. She walked around Bettie's room and spritzed on some perfume. "You work a lot for Bunny. Do you like her?"

Bettie gathered her things and went into the kitchen to make herself a picnic lunch. "Bunny takes incredible pictures of me. She knows lots of tricks like having me stand on a piece of wood buried in the sand so my entire foot shows instead of getting cut off." Bettie took a loaf out of the bread box and got grape jelly out of the frig. "She's like the perfect dance partner. We just know how to move and work together intuitively."

"True," said Goldie. She studied a proof print Bunny had sent over with an X over each image she had sold and the title of the magazine. "I thought she was kind of bossy."

Bettie shrugged and spread peanut butter on Wonder Bread. "She's a typical artist. Bunny loves Bunny. It is funny. She keeps calling me an 'unknown' and telling me how she is going to make my career."

"You mean she's never seen your magazine work? Doesn't she know 'Page is the Rage' and 'Miss Irresistible,' as they call you?"

Bettie licked the peanut butter off her fingertip and put some oranges in her bag. She added *The Long Goodbye*, Raymond Chandler's latest pocketbook, to kill the down time. "You'll get a kick out of this. The other day, she told me: 'I recognize the same qualities and creativity in you that I have myself. When I photograph you, I am expressing myself with your body.'"

Goldie rolled her eyes. "Geez. You would think she would pay you better since you are an extension of her magnificence." She held up a make-up kit. "Didn't she give you this three-dollar kit as payment for your last shoot?"

"I told you, she takes great photos." Bettie flipped through the proof sheets and pointed to a picture of her kneeling beside a white Christmas tree. She wore a Santa hat and winked at the camera as she held up an ornament. "Look at this one." Goldie whistled. "I just know she's going to find someone important to sell this one to."

Bettie was right about the quality of Bunny's photos, but she was so sweet-natured that she couldn't see that Bunny was a narcissist.

The modern psychological diagnosis of narcissism comes from the tale of Narcissus, in which I deliver justice. The story starts with Hera in a jealous rage. Unusual, I know.

Echo was a bubble-headed nymph that lived in the forest. Zeus began having an affair with one of her sisters, and he asked Echo to distract Hera if she came looking for him.

One day, Hera came snooping, and Echo met her, eager to share the latest gossip. As she prattled on and on, Zeus made his escape. Unfortunately for Echo, Hera spied her wayward husband making his get-a-way.

"You have tried to distract me," shouted Hera. "As punishment for your chatter, from this day on, you will only be able to repeat what others say, and never form a sentence of your own." Then she raced up to Mt. Olympus to rage against her cheating husband.

Echo wandered the forest. She felt isolated from her sisters because of her inability to talk. One day, she spied a handsome young man hunting. His name was Narcissus. Echo came out of the woods and smiled invitingly.

Startled, Narcissus demanded, "Who are you?"

"You," repeated Echo in the same tone of voice.

"Get away," he said, pointing his finger.

"Get away," said Echo. Trying to make her body show her true intentions, she kissed him.

He shoved her. "I would rather die than let you kiss me!"

"Kiss me," said Echo and fell to the ground weeping. Feeling no pity, Narcissus ran out of the forest. Heart-broken, Echo refused to eat and soon wasted away. She lives on as an echo in the hillsides.

I was furious for Narcissus' treatment. "By rejecting love, he has insulted me," I declared and cursed him. "From now on Narcissus will love only himself."

The next day, Narcissus knelt beside a pond to drink. As he leaned over the water, he saw his own reflection and fell madly in love. When he reached out to touch the beautiful face that stared back, his image disappeared in the ripples of water. Narcissus could not take his eyes off the image. He lay beside the pond and spoke words of love. The image mouthed the words but remained silent.

Soon Narcissus wasted away too. A second victim of unrequited love. I changed his body into a white flower called the Narcissus which grows beside water and bends over it, seeking its own reflection.

Although Narcissus got his just desserts, I suspected that Bunny would prosper. Modern society rewards the self-promoter. Bunny would bill herself as "the world's prettiest photographer" and pretend that she made Bettie, instead of acknowledging that Bettie made her.

15

Movie-Rama

Bettie returned to New York and the photographers continued to book her for magazine work. She enrolled in Herbert Berghof's acting studio to learn the Stanislavsky Method. I thought the classes were fascinating. I loved learning how an actor must search for inner motives to justify action.

The acting classes naturally extended to her modeling work. I liked to think that it was me supplying Bettie with her inner motive. I motivated her to play the Natural, and seduce through carefree joy, but also to be the Vixen.

I coached her how to became a powerful male fantasy.

Portray a highly sexual, supremely confident, alluring female who offers endless pleasure and a hint of danger.

I knew that in this post-WWII world, men longed for adventure and risk but had no outlets. Men had to always appear rational and conservative. Bettie offered a friendly, smiling face that might belong to their wife. Yet, at the same time, she presented a highly confident and sexual presence that was nothing like their spouse.

She learned how to seduce through calculated body poses and facial expressions––to portray the sexy girl next door who did naughty things in private.

Her acting classes were one of the main reasons she performed so well in her films. In addition to still photos, the Klaws had branched out into eight millimeter and sixteen millimenter short films called loops that were five to eight minutes long. They started off with dancing loops, with Bettie dancing alone.

"I feel so awkward," she called out during a shot. The films had no sound, so she could talk through a smile. "It is hard to dance without music, and I don't have any formal dance training."

"You're doing great, kid," called Irving Klaw as he watched through the lens. "Just keep that amazing smile and look like you're having fun."

It was much easier for Bettie to perform in the bondage-oriented loops. Irving called the two actresses over and critiqued their latest film. "Look at Bettie's face in this scene. She really looks like she is suffering and in pain. Patricia, you're the one spanking her, and you look like you are just playing patty cake." He pointed to the vacant look in Patricia's eyes and how she was obviously not exerting herself with the spank. "Get into the role. Make it believable. Bettie, can you give tips?"

Bettie made an 'aww shucks' motion with her hand and humbly explained what she did.

"I think of the Stanislavski Acting approach and try and feel at one with the role both mentally and physically." She played with her hair as she explained, "I don't do this kind of stuff in real life. So instead of staying in my head, I let the actions of the scene––getting spanked, tied up and gagged––form my inner image."

"Huh?" Patricia said, smacking her gum. Irving shot her a glance, and she spit it out into the nearest trash can.

"It's called the 'Magic If.' The actor needs to imagine themselves in a fictional circumstance and focus entirely on the fictional world of the drama. Don't allow yourself to be distracted by the camera crew, the audience, or personal concerns." Bettie looked from Patricia to Irving to see if she had made herself understood.

Irwin nodded, and Patricia bit on her lower lip. "I think I sort of get what you mean," she said. "Let's film it again, and I'll try and do better," she said. They went on and finished *Hobbled in Kid Leather Harness* which was released with Irving's approval.

Bettie was the star and the advertisements prominently displayed her name in the description. She worked with different girls and filmed other loops with overly descriptive titles including *Negligee Fight* and *Betty Gets Bound and Kidnapped.* She also appeared in several Burlesque films including *Striporama* and *Teaserama.*

The most fun she had was filming outdoors for a wealthy client of Irving's. They drove to his mansion in upstate New York which had large, manicured grounds to use as a location.

They shot several loops. In one film, Bettie and Roz Greenwood gagged and tied up another girl. They put her into a trunk of their car, slamming the lid with dominant scowls. In another, they tied their submissive to a tree. Bettie had no trouble inhabiting the evil character intent on forcing the innocent victim into obedience.

"What is it with all the bondage?" Roz asked between takes. "Can't we do something else but tie each other up?"

Bettie laughed and brushed her hair. "Men love to see women tied up and looking helpless."

"They also love to see you fight with each other—slapping and pulling hair," added Paula Klaw, as she untied the ropes from the actress.

"I think it's because they know in their guts that we women have tremendous power. Look how easy it is to control them with sex," Bettie said, as she reapplied her red lipstick. "Men might try and shame us and make us helpless, but someday we'll show them," said Bettie and turned to the girls with a raised fist.

I hoped Bettie was right. Throughout the centuries, I've inhabited many different women and tried to get them to recognize and seize their power.

The women on the set laughed companionably while the men stayed silent.

Bettie heard someone clear his throat and turned to look. It was the owner of the mansion, who looked chastened by what he had heard. Bettie flashed him a smile and patted him on his arm. "Not all men are alike, of course. Some are good eggs."

Smitten, he smiled back at her and announced, "Come take a break and visit my bar. I've made special tiki drinks for all of you."

#

Bettie's hunch that the Santa hat photo would find a good buyer was correct. Bunny sent the image to Hugh Hefner. He purchased the photo for his magazine *Playboy* and published the centerfold.

Hugh Hefner was inhabited by one of my favorite deities, Dionysus. He is the God of Wine, Pleasure, Festivity, Madness and Wild Frenzy. He throws the best parties.

I have to admit that Dionysus was not subtle with Hef. Dionysus was famous for his pinecone tipped staff, drinking cup, and long robe, and cloak. As Hefner, he replaced his staff with an ever-present pipe, often held a highball glass, and replaced his long robe with silk pajamas, and a bathrobe.

As a god, Dionysus had been followed by Mainades and satyrs. The Mainades were wild female followers of Dionysus. They would leave their homes, with their mixing-bowls standing full, and creep off into the woods. While there, they would dance in a wild frenzy, drink wine, and indiscriminately sleep with men. I think they were inspired more by me and my love of sex, but they hid it behind a worship of Dionysus. Clearly, Hefner had replaced his Mainades with Playboy Bunnies and, like Dionysus, was with them all night, alluring them with joyful mysteries.

The satyrs had been half-goat, half-man wood nymphs. They were lovers of wine, music, dancing, and women. They had "satyr play" which consisted of bawdy jokes and obscene behavior. Greek art often shows them with giant, permanent erections, frequently masturbating. As time went on, culture replaced the rough and lewd satyrs with gentle fauns that appeared in children's literature, stripped of all their masculinity.

Hefner, through Dionysus, knew that modern men were fauns. Their true desires had been repressed by society and they were sexually insecure and immature. Hefner created his Playboy empire to turn them back into the satyrs that lurked within. Hefner became a *bon vivant*, a person who enjoys a sociable and luxurious lifestyle, and his magazines encouraged his audience to become *bon vivants* as well. His lifestyle with the playmates demonstrated sexual liberation and freedom of expression. Dionysus replaced "satyr play" with the "Playboy Ethic," which said sex was a legitimate part of a sophisticated lifestyle.

Dionysus was on a personal mission to fight the Puritan ethic of America. Speaking through Hefner, he said, "Celebrate your life. Free it up. Your sexuality can be as good as anybody else's if you take the inhibitions out."

Modern men flocked to his magazine, pretending they read it for the articles. Their inner satyrs responded to the message that sex was pleasure to be enjoyed, not something dark to be sought illicitly.

It was message that both Bettie and I agreed with. We were both thrilled with the *Playboy* centerfold and knew it would help expand her modeling and acting options.

16

A Year to Remember

Ninteen-fifty-five was the best of times, and it was the worst of times for Bettie. Her year started off as Miss January in *Playboy's Holiday Issue*. Then the Earl Wilson T.V. show awarded Bettie with the title "Miss Pin Up Girl of the World."

Publication in *Playboy* had helped raise her status in the modeling world. The Men's Magazines that were Bettie's bread and butter, *Pose, Peep, Bold, Dare*, were considered lewd and they treated sex as a vice. However, *Playboy* was associated with class and sophistication, and Hefner's editorial content presented sex as a normal part of life.

Then trouble arrived in the form of Eris, the sister and constant companion of Ares. Remember her from Thetis' wedding? Her official title was the Goddess of Discord, and she was known for sowing contention and rivalry. Her mother was Nyx, the Goddess of Night, who gave birth, without a husband, to Eris and her other lovely children including Thanatos (Death), Oizys (Misery), Nemesis (Envy), Apate (Deceit), Epiales (Nightmares), and Geras (Old Age). Needless to say, Eris and her siblings tormented humans. I knew her well,

158

and told Ares I wouldn't make love with him unless he distanced himself from his horrible sister.

Even with Ares banishment, Eris refused to leave us alone until I agreed to give her back her golden Apple of Discord which I had won, fair and square, through the Judgement of Paris. I threw it at her. She caught it, and left us alone. However, Eris harbored a grudge against me.

Now, she was back. Eris thrives on war, and the end of WWII had left her feeling small and insignificant. The prosperity and optimism of midcentury America stuck in her craw. Her apple makes her grow large and feel important, so Eris tossed her Apple of Discord into the growing sexual freedom of America. It rolled through society, gathered momentum in the world of politics, and stopped at the feet of Irving Klaw.

To assist his sister in her game, Ares inhabited an ambitious senator from Tennessee by the name of Estes Kefauver. As the God of War, Ares was tall and handsome. I wouldn't call Kafauver handsome, but he was tall and emitted a kind of wholesome earnestness with his horn-rimmed glasses and coon-skin cap. He was seen as a Southern Jimmy Stewart—an atypical role for Ares but not entirely. Like Ares, he was vain and ambitious. Despite his "aw-shucks" hillbilly role, Kafauver was a womanizer. His nickname on Capitol Hill was "the Claw" for his habit of groping women in the Senate elevator. His favorite companions were Phobos (Fear) and Momos (Blame).

The senator had already felt the thrill of fame in 1950, when he chaired the US Senate Special Committee to Investigate Crime in Interstate Commerce. Hearings were held in fourteen major cities across the U.S., with more than six hundred witnesses testifying. Sponsored by *Time Magazine*, the hearings were televised live and featured notorious mob bosses. An estimated 30 million people tuned in to watch, and this made Senator Kefauver a nationally-recognized figure.

Now Kefauver was making a second bid for president, and he knew he needed the publicity of another investigative committee. What could garner more attention than the Mafia? Sex! The topic of his new hearings was the link between obscene and pornographic materials and juvenile delinquency. Under the auspices of protecting the children, Kefauver targeted comic books, lewd pin-ups, and fetish photographs.

Knowing that Eris still held her grudge, and Ares clung to his anger over our last breakup, I used my omniscient powers to keep an eye on the hearings. Senator Kefauver presided as the Chair. The lead manager, Mr. Gaughan, called an expert witness to the stand, Dr. George W. Henry, psychiatrist from Cornell University Medical College.

"Doctor, would you tell us what is a fetish?" Mr. Gaughan asked.

"A fetish is usually some object, material, or substance which becomes the chief source of sexual stimuli for a particular person."

"In your medical textbook entitled *All the Sexes*, you state that high-heel fetish and womens-lingerie fetish are two of the more common types," said Mr. Gaughan. "But tell me, Doctor, is there also a fetish known as bondage, in which people are trussed up?"

"Yes, that is fairly common in the group of sexual deviates."

Mr. Gaughan feigned shock as he continued. "You mean they like to see pictures of someone who is bound up?" The doctor nodded. "And some of them might like to be bound up themselves?"

"Yes, some like to be tied and some prefer to tie others. Bondage is often accompanied by whipping with actual whips, straps, sticks, and sometimes hairbrushes. This is a form of sadism and masochism."

Mr. Gaughan picked up a folder from his table and walked back to the front. "Dr. Henry, I am going to ask you to identify a number of pictures that I am going to produce as an exhibit here today."

The manager recorded the booklet, *Cartoons and Model Parade*, published by Irving Klaw, into the record. "I specifically call your attention to the advertisement for a movie offered by Klaw entitled *Negligee Fight*. Doctor, is this a form of the sadism or masochistic type of perversion in which two females can get erotic pleasure from fighting?"

Dr. Henry studied the ad for Bettie's sixteen millimeter film and said, "That is true."

"On page 7 of this publication, I direct you to this heading that says there are forty-four different bound-and-gagged photographs, eight being spanked, for forty cents apiece. It also offers seventy-one different high-heel and lingerie photos of models wearing six-inch high-heel shoes, bras and panties, at twenty-five cents." The manager paused. "Doctor, is it a fair statement to say that these pictures are for the purpose of exciting people to take part in the fetish?"

"Yes." Dr. Henry took the booklet from Gaughan's outstretched hand. He flipped through the pages, many of which contained images of Bettie.

"Can you find any other purpose for publishing such a booklet than for the erotic stimuli of people who will read it, and dwell upon it, and study it?"

"No, the sole purpose is to stimulate people erotically in an abnormal way."

"Doctor, could children be sexually perverted by looking at, by studying, and by dwelling upon photos of this nature and the contents of this book?"

"Yes, absolutely," said Dr. Henry.

Mr. Gaughan displayed a board that contained newspaper clippings from the Miami Daily News, dated August 31, 1954. He read the headlines aloud, "Coral Gables boy, Kenneth Grimms, found hanged. Weird death baffles cops. Father discovers body in trees." He gestured towards a man sitting in the audience. "I would like to announce at this point, the father of the boy is with us this morning and has been so kind as to consent to testifying following Dr. Henry's testimony."

He pointed to the newspaper clippings and then took out a police photograph. "The picture at which I am looking shows two saplings, with forks, and a 1x2 inch board suspended between the two forks of the tree. Hanging by his knees and, of course, in an inverted position, is Kenneth Grimm. The boy's ankles are tied with a rope, the same rope reaches from his ankles to his arms, and is looped around his neck, so that it bends his body in a sharp backward arc––a very grotesque-looking position."

Mr. Gaughan passed the photo to the other members of the hearing. "Doctor, I ask you is it in your opinion, from looking at this picture, would you say this is the end result of a sex crime? Does this impress you as the type of thing that can happen as the result of bondage—this fetish we have been discussing this morning?"

"Yes. It is an end result, a kind of result," said the Doctor to the room which had been shocked into silence.

Mr. Gaughan dismissed Dr. Henry after a few more questions and then called the dead boy's father, Clarence Grim, to testify.

"Thank you for cooperating with us." He then asked the father to describe, in detail the discovery of his son's body.

"He was trussed up in a very unnatural position. He wasn't hung like most people hang themselves by the neck from a rope. The fact that he didn't have any clothes on, and he was a modest boy, led me immediately to believe that there was some sex angle to it, some sex act in some way. It is still a mystery to me."

"Do you recognize, sir, this booklet which I hand you, entitled, *Cartoon and Model Parade*, published by Irving Klaw––the Pin-Up King?"

"Yes," said Mr. Grimm accepting the book.

"Would you tell the subcommittee how you first came upon a copy of this book?"

"With a mutual friend, I was puzzling over my son's death. He brought me a girlie-magazine and pointed to an advertisement for this booklet. I could see it had similar acts of tying people up that reminded me of my son's case. That is why we sent off for it."

Mr. Gaughan discussed various images in Klaw's book and asked the father to compare his son's bondage with the models. Then he said, "This picture here shows a model known as Bettie Page." His fingers traced the ropes, "Does that accurately reflect how your boy was found?

"It is more or less the same. It is a very similar position; there is a resemblance to the way I found him," said Mr. Grimm.

"In other words, when you went through this book by yourself, you were immediately struck by the number of illustrations in that book that depicted the same fashion in which your boy died," declared Mr. Gaughan to the hearing.

The father tried to remain stoic but his voice cracked. "The way that he was tied, it wasn't anything that any youngster like him, with his character—it wasn't anything that he could concoct himself. There wasn't any history of that—no similar action on his part. He was active in the Boy Scouts from the time he was a little bit of a fellow. He had attended a boys' camp in Tennessee for five or six seasons. He had only been home two days from the camp when this happened." Mr. Grimm took several deep breaths before continuing.

"Therefore, I feel that he couldn't have thought of anything like that. It would have had to have been brought to his attention by either someone else showing him how, or showing him a picture of it—I don't know. I feel there is a definite connection between this sort of thing and his death. I also feel there is definitely an evil to this. It isn't good. It is an unhealthy situation. It is not wholesome.

There is nothing cultural about it. It is just no damned good. That is all I can say about it."

#

Two representatives from Senator Kefauver's committee showed up at Bettie's front door. "You are required to testify against Irving Klaw, and admit what you know about his pornography business."

"Pornography? Irving never even shot nudes. He would make us wear two pairs of panties if they were sheer to make sure there was never any pubic hair showing. We never even showed nipples. No men. No sex acts. No open legged poses. Irving knew the definition of pornography, and he was always careful."

Despite her protests, she was summoned to the U.S. Courthouse in New York. They forced her to wait, alone, in a small room.

"I won't testify against Irving. I refuse to lie and call his photographs pornography," Bettie shouted as they led her into the room.

"We will see what the Senator decides. You will wait here in the meantime."

I argued in her mind, trying to help her prepare a defense.

What is salacious and obscene? There is no clear definition. It is just society that treats sex as shameful, guilty, taboo-ridden. You aren't guilty for not agreeing with their Puritan attitudes.

Bettie paced the floor of the room. "I think they are being perfectly awful to Irving. He is such a nice man. I hope they don't try and make me seem like some victim. I always felt safe with Paula tying me up. I knew she would never do anything to hurt me."

I recognized the Apple of Discord at work. Society was loosening up. Kinsey had issued a second report, *Sex and the American Female*, and conversations were finally happening about the true nature of sex. At the same time, the results of his study on female sexuality was greeted with far more outrage and criticism than his book on the male had garnered. The old double-standard at work again.

Women weren't supposed to enjoy sex, and there was something wrong with those that did.

Remember, those politicians are playing to the moralists, crabbed repressed types that croak about the evils of the seducer. Secretly they envy our power. We live according to our own heart and morals. We don't need to concern ourselves with others opinions.

I reminded Bettie, hoping she would stay strong and not crack under the strain.

There are three great enemies of sexual expression—–shame, repression, and silence. Don't surrender to any of these.

At the end of 16 hours, police opened the door and let Bettie go without asking her to testify or answer a single question.

#

Irving Klaw, however, was forced to testify. Boxes of his negatives and photographs were presented into evidence.

"Our investigation reveals that Mr. Klaw is one of the largest distributors of obscene, lewd, and fetish photographs throughout the country by mail. We have had testimony today as well as last week, showing the effect that these photographs have on juveniles and on youth." The manager held up a list. "We have in our investigation determined information to that effect that he has a list—–"

Senator Kefauver interrupted him, "You mean that he uses young people or minors in the pictures?"

"No. He has a mailing list of the customers that order his photographs. Sixty-five percent of that mailing list are girls from six to sixteen years of age," said the manager.

Mr. Klaw's attorney intervened. "Mr. Klaw sells images of movie stars to the girls on that list. Remember he runs *Movie Star News*. Mr. Klaw, and his sister Paula, buy publicity photos from the Hollywood studios and sell them to the customers on that mailing list."

"Mr. Klaw, describe all aspects of the business you are in," said the Mr. Gaugan.

"I decline to answer under the fifth amendment of the Constitution, that to answer may tend to incriminate me," said Klaw.

The manager reworded the question and was met with the same response. Regardless of the question, Klaw declined to answer and pled the Fifth.

"Mr. Klaw, in fairness and in compliance with the requirements of the Supreme Court, I must warn you that this committee will cite you for contempt of the Senate if you decline to answer, and I will now give you a further chance to answer," shouted Senator Kefauver, furious that the hearing was not going as planned.

In the end, Kefauver was unable to provide any evidence linking Klaw to charges of obscenity. There was no proof that the murder victim, Kenneth Grimm, had ever seen *Cartoon and Model Parade*. There was no evidence that the juvenile girls who ordered movie star pictures from Klaw ever received anything other than those pictures.

In the end, Senator Kefauver dismissed Klaw and the others he had charged with pornography. His exposé had failed, as did his presidential bid.

The notoriety of the trial, and the mention of her name, boosted Bettie's career. Bunny Yeager's photos flooded the market and other photographers clamored to shoot Bettie and her winning smile.

However, police and authorities continued to hound Klaw through postal code regulations. Irving Klaw reminded me of Prometheus. It seemed as though he would be eternally punished for daring to give people a forbidden gift. His gift was an open-mindedness towards sexuality and eroticism. A gift that lay outside the bounds of what the gods of society deemed normal and therefore must be punished.

Prometheus was the Titan who stole fire from the gods and gave it to humankind. Zeus was furious because he feared the power of fire would elevate mortals to the role of gods. As his first punishment, he ordered Hephaestus to create a woman from clay. Zeus brought her to life and named her Pandora and sent her to earth as the wife of Epimetheus, Prometheus' brother. Pandora means "all gifts" and she was beautiful, graceful, sexy, and talented. For her wedding, she received a box with the warning, "Do not open." How could anyone, god or mortal, resist? She opened the box and all of Nyx's children flew out. The Gods of Death, Misery, Envy, Deceit and Old Age—remember them?

Horrified, Pandora slammed the lid on the box and Hope was trapped. This is why Hope remains the most powerful weapon against the ills of the world. Just like Eve in the *Bible*, the fault of all the ills in the world were caused by a woman not obeying the rules. The gods of society considered Bettie, and models like her, to be modern day Pandoras.

Zeus did not stop his punishment with Pandora, he captured Prometheus and chained him to a rock. Hephaestus created a robot in the form of an eagle, Zeus' symbolic bird. Zeus imbued it with eternal life and a purpose. The raptor pecked out Prometheus' liver. The liver is the seat of emotion, so the torture was both physical and mental. The anguish was unbearable, but Prometheus was immortal, so he could bear it. He sighed with relief when the eagle finished eating and flew away.

However, his immortal body healed and his liver grew back overnight. In the morning, the eagle arrived for another feast. This continued for eternity as a warning for anyone who tried to give gifts that humans were not entitled to.

Like Prometheus, Klaw would be punished and made into an example. Every time he tried to get back into the photography business, the enforcers of society would find a way to shut him down. The man who owned the printing lab also worked for Disney, and was warned to stop doing business with the Klaws. Impromptu raids and inspections made models, even in innocent poses, nervous about working with him. Police destroyed over seventy-five percent of his photographs and negatives. In 1957, exhausted from the harassment, with his health declining from the unrelenting stress, Irving stopped photographing pin-ups.

Irving called Bettie to break the news. "Look, we have a little problem with the federal government. We aren't going to shoot anymore. I don't want you to think that I'm not calling you for work because we don't like you. You know we love you. I don't want you to get involved. I want to protect you."

"Oh Irving, I'm so sorry this has happened to you. I want you to know how much I loved working with you and Paula. I'll never forget your kindness and support," Bettie said.

17

The Apple of Discord

Irving Klaw might have wanted to protect Bettie, but the Apple continued to roll through her life in 1957. It started simply enough, with a white envelope in the mail. Bettie frowned, as she realized there was no return address, but opened it. The letter was typewritten and unsigned.

Dear Bettie,

You always smile in your pictures, no matter how you are posed. I'm going to wipe that smile off of your face. I know where you live, and I watch your apartment. One night, I'm going to grab you and tie you up and shove a ball in your mouth. Then I'm going to carve my initials in your pretty little ass. I'll paint you with your own blood. Once you are begging me to stop, I'll pull that ball out of your mouth and shove my dick down your throat. I'll fuck your mouth until tears come out of your eyes and you gag. Then I'll put the ball back and save you for later.

"Oh my God," she whispered, tossing the offending letter onto the floor. I felt her heart palpitating and anxiety flooding her system. I tried to calm her.

I'm sure this letter doesn't mean anything. It is probably because of the publicity of the Klaw hearing. They mentioned your name specifically, and I'll bet a bunch of people went out and looked up the bondage pictures.

Bettie jumped up and closed the curtains. She stood in the dark, shaking and wringing her hands. She had no close girl friends to call, and she was between boyfriends. She didn't want to add any burdens to the Klaws's plate so she decided to keep silent.

Her efforts at peace lasted for one day. The next day, and the next, and the next, more letters arrived. The contents grew more graphic with each one. The writer threatened, "I will tear your nipples off with pliers," and "I will tie you spread eagle and rape you until you bleed."

Bettie couldn't sleep. She jumped at every noise. The letter writer appeared to be tracking her movements. "Today I saw you at the Five and Dime. You bought yourself a Coke, and I watched you drink it with those pretty red lips." Another one said, "I saw you leaving all gussied up in a black dress. Are you going to a modeling job or to fuck another man? I don't like that. You don't want to know what I am capable of when I get mad."

Bettie refused all modeling requests and barely left the house. When she had to leave, she covered her face with black sunglasses, wore no make-up, and tied a scarf around her head. She wore flat shoes and baggy jeans, trying to do anything she could to not look sexy.

The letters continued. I gave up trying to deny the threat. Even in Ancient Greece, we had sickos. Men would come into my temples at night and masturbate on my ivory statues. The priests had to start every day by cleaning them. I was insulted by the disrespect, but the thought of experiencing what the stalker threatened through a mortal body terrified even me.

Finally, after two weeks, she called her Momma in tears and told her about the letters. "Come home, Honey. We need you out of the Big City."

#

Bettie went home to Nashville, hoping to find a safe haven, but unsure if she would find one. Her mother had always been reserved and not a shoulder to cry on. However, Bettie didn't have any other options. She was afraid to reach out to Goldie or her other siblings. They all had children, and she didn't want the maniac to turn his sights on them.

In recent years, her mother had found Jesus. In the guise of offering help, she made comments like, "The Lord might be telling you to stop your sinful ways. Those pictures are sins in the eyes of the Almighty."

You haven't done anything wrong. You are the victim, not the criminal.

Bettie could barely hear me. My voice was drowned out as she ruminated over the contents of every letter and played out all of the threats in her mind. Even though she was out of the City, she jumped at every sound and could barely sleep. She lost weight and her skin became sallow.

It didn't take long until Bettie was blaming herself too. "I hate to think what Jesus will do to me for all of my sins."

I felt like we were going backwards. Bettie had represented body pride and freedom from sexual conventions and, through the letters of one nut, she was reduced to shame and regret. I tried to use her own religion to reason with her.

Jesus gave you a beautiful body and he provided you with opportunities to share it with the world. You just posed naked—you didn't kill anyone.

It might surprise you that I can acknowledge other deities. I'm not threatened. I believe there are many paths to the top of the mountain, and I don't care which path a person takes. In Ancient Greece, when the army took over an area with a different religion, our priests took the attitude that their gods were just different names for us. Priests frequently incorporated the new deities in stories. This is one reason, scholars say, why Zeus had so many affairs and children. But I know that Zeus really is a randy alpha-male and that's just a nice explanation to excuse his promiscuity.

I didn't care that she was talking to Jesus, but I didn't like how she felt like she was guilty of sinning and deserved punishment.

Despite my reminding her of her innocence, Bettie prayed all night for forgiveness for her sins. The bondage, the nudes, the Camera Clubs, the sex outside of marriage, the divorce from Billy, the list went on and on throughout the sleepless nights. When she would finally fall asleep, Epiales, the brother of Eris, would ride in on his Night Mare.

In one nightmare, Bettie dreamed that she stood before God on trial. He delivered his verdict with a finger pointed directly at her. "You believe that your law is above my law; therefore, you shall be punished. I sentence you to be buried alive."

Naked, Bettie was led into an underground tomb and the lid was slid closed over the opening. She had one small lantern and enough food and water for three days. The tomb felt cold and the air held the metallic smell of wet stone. She looked at the flickering light and imagined the horror she would feel when the tomb plunged into darkness. Why should she live for three days in the dark, only to die of thirst?

Taking the sheets off her bed, she twisted them into a rope, threw one end over the slider that had closed the tomb's lid, and hung herself.

She gasped and woke up just as her body was reaching the end of its life. She was covered in sweat and shaking. The nightmare had felt so real. She could still smell the dankness of the tomb and feel the sheet-rope around her neck.

The next morning, Bettie told her mother about the dream.

Her mother gasped, "Taking your own life is an unpardonable sin. Deuteronomy 30:19 says 'I have set before you life and death, blessings and curses. Now chose life.'"

"I dreamed I killed myself; I didn't say I was going to do it. I just feel so trapped and suffocated. My life feels like a kind of death." Bettie broke into sobs. She longed to feel her mother's embrace and comfort, but she only heard more words.

"1 Corinthians 6:19-20 says 'Your body is a Temple of the Holy Spirit. You are not your own. Therefore, honor God with your body.' You defiled your Temple and now you are paying the price."

I knew we needed to get away from Momma. Here Bettie was being shamed for her dreams, on top of her past. Nothing good could come from staying, so I urged her to leave.

Maybe the letters stopped once you left town. You should go back to New York. Thankfully, Bettie agreed with me. I think her mother's condemnation had become almost as bad as the stalker.

She brushed her tears from her eyes. "Momma, I'm going to go back. I can't stay here."

Her mother nodded and didn't try to change her mind.

#

When we got home, her mailbox was stuffed with letters. The landlord handed her a rubber-banded stack and said, "You must be popular. Your box overflowed. Fan mail?"

Bettie nodded, feeling numb. She took the stack of letters upstairs and raced through the apartment, checking every closet, under the bed and behind the shower curtain. She sat on the couch trembling and stared at the pile of mail.

Don't open them. They're all the same envelope with no return address. Take them all to the police.

Bettie ignored me and opened each letter and read each word. She filled her mind with the images and fantasies of a sadistic lunatic.

"What can I do? The police won't help me. After all, it is my fault for my filthy pictures. They will think I deserve this." She held her face in her hands and cried. "I probably do." I shouted in her mind, trying to override her spiraling thoughts of despair.

Stop this! Do not blame yourself. This guy is crazy and, if he wasn't doing this to you, he'd do it to some other woman. You have to go to the police. Maybe he's done this before. At least try and stop him. Never give up.

"Even if they catch him, you know what will happen. In a trial, they will bring up my sexual history and bondage modeling to discredit me."

I begged Athena for wisdom. I begged her to supply me with the tactics that would help me win this war. Her inspiration arrived immediately.

The mail! The letters have been sent through the mail. Go to the FBI and not the local police. This is a pornographic threat sent through the mail. After those hearings they won't be able to ignore violation of postal regulations.

Bettie stopped crying and sat up. "The mail!" She collected all of the letters and put them into a paper bag. Then she dressed in her most conservative dress, the one she saved for funerals, and wore modest makeup—just enough to charm the FBI into helping her.

\#

Athena's strategy was right on the mark. I was worried that she would hold a grudge over me getting Bettie, but when she saw that the problems were caused by Eris and Ares, two gods she loathed, she was eager to join my team.

The local police and the FBI worked together. The FBI believed the letter writer was a murderer that had eluded capture. They planned a sting and asked for Bettie's help.

"We need you to start leaving the house. Make it look like you aren't scared any more. This will goad him into moving beyond letters," said the head agent.

He was right and in a few days a letter arrived demanding that she put specific bondage images of herself into an envelope and drop it off on the corner of One 116th Street and Amsterdam Avenue, at 2:00 p.m., the following Saturday. He warned her not to have anyone with her or to contact the police. He closed the letter with a gruesome description of what he would do to her if she didn't show up.

"Perfect," said the agent. "Don't worry. We'll get him."

On Saturday, Bettie stood on the appointed corner holding a large manila envelope. Six FBI agents hid in cars nearby. They waited 30 minutes, but no one appeared. Bettie worried that the nightmare would continue. Then, two teenage boys came out of an apartment building on the other side of the street, opposite the corner she stood on. They looked around and went back inside.

Two FBI agents followed them. They pounded on the apartment door and demanded entrance.

One of the boys, a lanky fellow with horn-rimmed glasses, opened the door and backed up when he saw the badges. "Phil?" He called to the boy over his shoulder.

Phil, short and muscle-bound, came to the door with false bravado. "What can I do for you?"

One of the agents brushed past the boys and began looking around the apartment. "Are your folks at home?"

"We—we are here alone, but I could call my dad at work," said the lanky boy.

The second agent held out one the last letter Bettie had received. "Which of you two wrote this letter?" The boys looked at each other, and Phil jerked his head forward, urging his friend to stay quiet.

"Look, you're both going to the station. Are you going to cooperate or make this difficult?"

The lanky boy folded instantly. "It was Phil's idea. He said we could have some fun and it wouldn't hurt anybody."

"You said some pretty graphic stuff in those letters," said the agent.

"You've seen all the letters?" The boy took off his glasses and wiped the sweat off his face.

"You think I can write like that? This guy's the straight-A student. We talked about it, but he's the author," shouted Phil.

"Come in here," called the agent from the back of the apartment. The other agent and boys followed his voice. He pointed to a typewriter. "This what you used?"

"Yep, that's it. Dust it for fingerprints. You'll see that he wrote them all," said Phil.

The agent nodded towards his partner, "We're taking you both in for questioning. You can call your folks at the station." He slapped handcuffs on Phil and his partner did the same to the other boy.

Bettie watched the agents exit the building with the boys. "Is that them?" She asked the agent who stood with her outside.

"Looks like it." He shook her hand, "Thank you for your cooperation, Miss Page. You can go home now. We'll be in touch."

After the sting, the letters stopped. It took a while, but eventually Bettie found her old spirit and began leaving the house again. She kept waiting to hear from the cops, but the court system moved slowly. Eventually, she learned that, since the boys were minors and had cooperated, there wouldn't be a trial. Their punishment for Bettie's trauma was three months of community service and a promise to refrain from such behavior in the future.

It's a disappointing sentence, but at least the letters stopped and you didn't have to testify at a trial.

"I just can't believe how young they were to be writing such sick things." Bettie took a deep breath and let it out. "I'm sick of hearings and trials and attention. I'd be happy to be an invisible nobody."

#

Bettie tried to resume her career. She agreed to photo shoots in bikinis, but refused to do any more nudity.

"I look old," she said and pointed to the wrinkles around her eyes in a magazine photo.

I didn't try and talk her out of her assessment. It wasn't just that she was thirty-four years old, it was that she didn't look like she was having fun anymore. Her smile looked forced. She had lost her passion and the camera didn't lie.

"There are so many pictures of me out there. Seven years' worth. I don't know why anyone would still want to photograph me," she said as she looked in the mirror and pulled on her skin to hide the wrinkles. "But the money is so good that it would be hard to stop."

#

A second stalker appeared six months later. I cursed Eris. Every time someone tries to fight against the Apple of Discord, it grows bigger. I feared that this is what had happened when Bettie attempted to resume modeling instead of admitting defeat.

This time it was a thirty year old white man. He wore a black suit and black horn-rimmed glasses. Every day, he stood across the street from her apartment for hours, looking up at her window. He never approached the building, but it went on for two weeks. At my urging, Bettie finally decided to call the police. But I suspect Eris had already had her fun, and the man didn't appear again.

Bettie began making plans to leave New York and stop modeling. She wanted to stay until her lease ran out, but Eris pushed her hand.

Police knocked on the door with hard firm raps early one morning.

Bettie pulled her robe tighter around herself and opened the door, peeking around the edge as the two officers showed her their badges.

"Please let us in, Miss Page. We need your assistance in a pornography case."

Bettie opened the door and invited the officers to sit down. An agent spread images out on her coffee table. "These pornographic photos were sold to an undercover cop. We want to hear your side of the story."

Bettie looked at the photos and shame filled her. They were from that night, so many years ago, when she had gotten drunk on blackberry brandy with the Camera Club men. She knew the photos fit the definition of pornography. Pubic hair was the least of it. In one photo, her legs were spread wide open, showing her clitoris. In another, her finger touched herself as though masturbating.

She hid her eyes in shame. "I know you won't believe me, but this happened the only night in my life that I have ever been drunk." She looked up and the agent nodded encouragingly. "It was after a Camera Club shoot. Some guys took me to a party, but it turned out to be just them. I got drunk on blackberry brandy. It was so delicious and sweet. I didn't realize how tipsy I had gotten. The men told me to pose and," she gestured towards the photos, "I followed their directions."

The agent cleared his throat. "Actually, we do believe you. The events were the same as those told by the man who tried to sell these photos. He said he was ashamed––that he knew the models trusted the photographers. He said that he'd known it was wrong––taking the photos because you were so drunk, and that he hadn't wanted to sell them, but he'd borrowed money from a loan shark, and was desperate to pay him back."

"Will I go to jail?" Bettie asked.

"No. The guilt lies with the photographer. We consider the model a victim. You won't be punished."

Bettie breathed a sigh of relief. "Thank you. These photos? Will they be destroyed?"

"The guy pled guilty so there won't be a trial, if that is what you are worried about. We will keep them in the vault as evidence. But no one in the public will see them." The officers rose and shook Bettie's hand. "Thank you for your cooperation."

After they left, Bettie shot the three dead bolts across her door and leaned against it. She made her decision.

She picked up the phone and called Paula Klaw. After catching up on small talk and inquiring after Irving's failing health, Bettie said, "I just wanted you to know. I've quit modeling for good. I'm moving to Florida."

18

Aphrodite Exits

Bettie moved down to Florida, near her sister, Goldie. She told her about the stalkers and warned her to be vigilant. Bettie had always been frugal and had savings to live off. She kept to herself and lived a small life.

I knew my opportunity to use Bettie as a vehicle for sexual freedom and body love had come to a close. Through her, I had come so close to freeing American women from their shame and prudishness. I had started conversations about sex, just like Hermes was doing through Tennessee Williams, and Dionysius was doing through Hugh Hefner. We were challenging Puritan values.

However, the Kefauver hearings against Klaw, and the stalking incidents forced me to admit defeat. America wasn't ready to change. I felt like Sisyphus, punished for trying to change the natural order of things.

Sisyphus was a wily trickster who twice cheated death. The first time he died, he entered Hades and was able to capture and chain up Thantos, the God of Death. With Thantos out of commission,

Sisyphus went back up to earth and no humans could die. The gods couldn't tolerate this, so Ares freed Thantos and reestablished mortality for humans.

The second time Sisyphus died, he cried to Persephone in the Underworld that his wife had buried him without the proper sacrifices and offerings. He promised to return to Hades, if she would just let him out to take care of the rituals. Persephone never lost her naivety and let him out. Needless to say, Sisyphus didn't return. Unobtrusively, he lived to be an old man.

However, the third time he died, Zeus decided to make an example of Sisyphus because he didn't want other mortals thinking they could cheat death.

Zeus forced Sisyphus to roll an enormous boulder up a steep hill in Hades, promising that once he reached the top and pushed it over, he would be freed. Sisyphus wrestled the huge rock with both hands, braced his feet, and took a single step. Struggling and straining, he pushed the boulder uphill. However, just as he reached the top, where one push would have sent it over, the weight of the boulder caused it to roll backwards down the hill again. Sisyphus had to start again. Zeus decreed his labors must last for eternity.

I too am forever pushing a boulder uphill. I have lived in other bodies throughout the ages and come close to creating societies that honored women, gave them control over their bodies, and allowed all people to express their sexuality the way that they see fit. But, like Sisyphus, I never manage to push the bolder over the top of the hill. The weight of morality, judgement, and shame causes the rock to roll back down to the bottom. Each time, I am forced to begin again, with a new mortal, and try and push it over the top.

Despite my defeat, I wasn't willing to exit Bettie. I was worried about her. I didn't think it would easy to give up her modeling career and become an invisible nobody. Eris and her Apple of Discord concerned me too. I didn't think she was done rolling it through Bettie's life.

#

On a sunny day, Bettie was sitting with Goldie in the backyard chatting and watching her children romp with their dog.

"I always regret not having kids," Bettie said.

Goldie stared at her with bugged-out eyes. "Since when?"

"Since, I left modeling. I have regrets and think maybe I should have been like you," she pointed at the kids. "Marriage, house, kids, dog."

Goldie reached over and pretended to wring her neck. "Are you crazy? You lived your life. You didn't end up another mom in the suburbs. Don't regret a thing."

Bettie gave a half-hearted smile and shrugged. I decided I needed to help her find a distraction to cheer her up.

Didn't Armond Walterson live here in Florida? Why not give him a call?

Bettie perked up and said to Goldie, "I'm thinking of looking up an old boyfriend down in Key West. Want to come with?"

#

Bettie felt like a stalker herself as she sat outside Armond's parents' house.

"I'm surprised you remembered where it was after four years," said Goldie. "What are we going to do? You don't even know if he still lives here."

"He'd be twenty-two, I hope he still doesn't live with his folks. Look, I can't risk his mom recognizing me, why don't you go up to the door and pretend to be a friend from high school."

"What high school did he go to?" asked Goldie as she prepared to leave the car.

"I don't remember. Just say you met him at the beach or something—be creative." She playfully shoved Goldie to get out.

Bettie sat in the car and watched as Goldie went up the sidewalk and rang the bell. Armond's mother answered the door, and Bettie sunk lower in the driver's seat. She saw the mom smile as she chatted with Goldie. She disappeared for a moment then returned with a piece of paper that she handed over.

Goldie skipped down the sidewalk and double-checked that the mom had closed the door before going over to Bettie.

"Got it! Here's his address and his phone number. Which shall we use?"

"Let's drive to his place and decide then," said Bettie as she turned on the engine and drove to the address.

Outside of Armond's apartment, the Page sisters sat in the car like a pair of undercover cops waiting for their suspect.

"This is boring. Let's ring the bell," complained Goldie.

"Let's wait a bit longer," said Bettie and as the words left her mouth, the door opened. Armond walked out first, handsome in plaid shorts and a golf shirt. "Yum, he's gotten better with age. Look at those shoulders. I think he's even taller," whispered Bettie.

"Uh-oh, who's the girl?" asked Goldie. A blonde, dressed in a darling golf skirt and matching top exited and turned to lock the door.

"Drat, of course he has a girlfriend. I should tell her that I'm the one who taught him everything he knows. She should thank me." Bettie started the engine.

"Don't give up so easy." Goldie pointed to the paper. "Maybe she isn't the girl of his dreams—call him and see if he wants more lessons from his old teacher."

That evening, Bettie called Armond's number. He answered and Bettie's tummy curled at the sound of his deep voice.

"Hi, I don't know if you remember me. We dated about four years ago, and I'm in town now so I thought—"

"Bettie?" Armond interrupted, "Is it you?"

Nearly collapsing with relief, Bettie laughed. After filling him in with small talk and how she was doing, Bettie explained to Armond,

"Our ending was so abrupt, without even a goodbye. I always wondered how you were doing."

"Man, I wanted to kill my mom for the way she treated you. Listen, I never stopped thinking about you, Bet. No girl knows how to kiss like you. Kiss and do everything else." They laughed. "I'd love to see you again."

"Great. Um, are you single?" Bettie held her breath. If he lied, she knew she couldn't see him. She wouldn't lose her heart to a cheater like she had with Carlos.

"I've got a girl. Her name is Margaret. She's all right—great golfer, but I'll drop her like a hot potato if I can get you back in my arms."

Bettie's heart did a little happy dance as the two made plans for that evening.

#

Their reunion was magical. After dinner, the pair went straight to Bettie's place. He remembered everything she liked to do in bed, and had learned some new tricks. It didn't take long before they were an item.

Bettie worried about his mother, but Armond insisted she had the wrong idea about her. Once again, she was invited to dinner. This time, Bettie and Armond arrived together.

With his hand clasping hers, Armond opened his parents' door and called out, "Ma, we're home."

His mother came out from the kitchen with an apron tied around her waist and her hair back in a scarf. She was prettier than Bettie had remembered. She reached her arms towards Bettie with a huge smile. "Armond says you are scared of me—don't be." She gave Bettie a warm hug. "Four years later and you are back in his life and he is as crazy for you as ever—it sounds like a relationship that was meant to be. I want you to feel welcome in this family."

Warmth flooded Bettie. She'd always wanted to be part of a big, happy family. "Thank you, it means so much."

Armond's family was bigger than Bettie could imagine, he had eleven brothers and sisters. Bettie became a welcomed member of the clan and enjoyed their picnics on the beach, running sack races, and jumping rope. Every family gathering felt like a party.

Ten months after reuniting, Armond and Bettie got married at the First Methodist Church in downtown Key West. Goldie was her matron of honor, and Bettie wore a manila-colored silk dress that she made herself.

I was thrilled for Bettie and thought we would be happy living a domestic life with this easy-going man who was a generous lover. It wouldn't be exciting, but it would be comfortable.

#

Bettie got a job as a secretary in the Department of Public Works, and Armond worked as the head of shipping at the U.S. Naval Station. The couple tried to get pregnant, but month after month passed with no success. Bettie thought back to how hard she and Billy had tried, and how she'd never accidently gotten pregnant, despite a few condom accidents with lovers.

"I guess it must be me that is infertile," she thought.

You can have a rich life without children. Enjoy yourself with Armond.

Fortunately, the family picnics gave Bettie plenty of time to be around Armond's nieces and nephews. Between them and Goldie's kids, Bettie started to realize she didn't really want to be a mother. It looked like a lot of thankless work.

Secretarial work kept her busy, and Armond and Bettie bought a boat and spent their weekends sailing. Unfortunately, that old restless feeling didn't take long to resurface in Bettie.

"He never wants to dance, and he's afraid to travel."

Even when he does dance, he has two left feet. But, he's a good man with a great family.

"We only have three things in common: movies, sex and hamburgers. Hamburgers, hamburgers, hamburgers! That's all he wants me to cook and that's the only kind of restaurant we can go out to."

I'm not a huge fan of marriage myself, but I honestly believed Armond would be the best way for Bettie to transition into a new life. I didn't want her to give up on him.

Marriage is challenging. You've been independent for so long it might take a while to settle into it. Be patient.

"He's so much younger than me and so boring."

I knew Bettie was looking for something to fill the void in her life. She reminded me of a soldier returning home from war. The modeling had been exciting and filled with different photographers and experiences. But the hearings and stalking episodes had created a type of post-traumatic stress syndrome. She was trying to get back on track with her life by doing safe things like work and marriage, but she still carried the scars of those experiences. I thought time would heal her and never anticipated what happened next.

#

On New Year's Eve, Bettie got dressed up to go out, but stopped when she saw Armond sitting on the couch in his T-shirt and underwear.

"You need to get ready, if we don't hurry up all the clubs will be full," she said.

"I'm not going out. I hate those crowds," Armond said and scratched his privates.

"But you promised." Bettie stomped her high-heel. "I told you it was my tradition to dance the New Year in and you agreed to go out,"

Armond shrugged. "I'm not going. You'll make me stay on that dance floor all night like the last time I gave into you. I'll just feel awkward." He looked over at her. She had her arms crossed and her lips pursed. He stood up and kissed her. "Besides, we can ring in the

New Year our special way." He pulled her tight to continue to his seduction, but Bettie wriggled out of his arms like a fish.

"Why can't you have a little fun for once?" She demanded.

Armond gave up placating Bettie. He turned up the T.V. and returned to the couch. "You're married now. You ought to learn how to settle down and stay home like a wife." He waved his hand in dismissal.

That gesture made Bettie's blood boil. She left the room and took off her party dress and shoes. She left them in a pile on the floor and changed into a sweater and pants. I didn't understand her anger and the feeling of desperation that I could feel racing through her.

"I never should have married him. There has to be more to life than this."

Calm down. Why are you so angry? This is your first fight as a couple. Go out there and make up with him.

"No. I'm going to do what I want, when I want." Bettie put on her shoes, combed her hair and grabbed her purse. She walked into the living room and headed straight for the front door.

"Where are you going?" Armond demanded.

"I'm going to the beach. I guess I'll spend New Year's Eve wishing upon a star, since I can't get any wishes granted in this house." She slammed out the door and started walking.

She walked quickly, her feet hitting the ground with force and her arms swinging. I felt that the beach was a good idea. The sound of the waves and the salt air would help Bettie find her center and hopefully stop this fight-or-flight I could feel in her.

Then, the strangest thing happened. A third voice appeared in Bettie's head. It was the deep voice of an old man, but it was infused with gentleness and love. The voice gave her directions.

"Cross the street," it said, and Bettie obeyed.

"Turn right at this corner." The voice kept directing her where to go, and Bettie obeyed like a robot. I tried to get her to stop and think.

Where are we going? I thought you wanted to go to the beach? Who is that voice?

Bettie ignored me and the voice continued to direct her. Finally, it told Bettie to stop.

"Look up," it said.

Bettie looked up and saw a white neon cross glowing over the top of a little church. Gospel music, accompanied by clapping, poured out the open doors. Bettie could feel the rhythm in her gut, just like when she heard jazz.

"Go inside. Hear the message," directed the voice.

Bettie entered the church and slipped into the back pew. The woman beside her gave her a friendly smile and edged towards her to share her hymnal. Bettie began singing and her heart lifted as the music poured through her.

When the song was over, she sat down and stared at the preacher giving the sermon. He was white and looked like a younger version of Billy Graham, whom Bettie had seen on T.V. His voice was rich and strong and penetrating. While he spoke, his eyes scanned the congregation, and Bettie felt his gaze single her out. She felt like he was speaking directly to her.

"Our heart is sinful. It is filled with evil imaginations of the wicked. Our hearts are filled with lust. God sees how you really are down inside. He sees your wickedness."

Bettie nodded her head, and I could feel the warmth of shame fill her.

Don't listen to this. Your heart isn't wicked. Let's get out of here.

"Shh," Bettie said to me, but she said it out loud and everyone in the church turned to look at her. She stared at the floor and blushed.

"Open yourself to the pain and let it sink into your heart. Do you have within yourself the spiritual resilience to change your wicked heart?" The preacher asked. "Are you ready to become a warrior and fight your own wickedness? There is a battle in your mind with lust. The Devil is your spiritual enemy and his goal is to steal, kill, and destroy. He wants to distract you with lust and pornography to take you out of this war. You must be a warrior and this is the sword you will raise in battle." The preacher lifted the Bible and thrust it towards the congregation.

Bettie nodded and a lump formed in her throat.

"The Bible was written in tears and to tears it will yield its best treasures," he said.

Bettie's mind filled with images of her nude modeling, the pornographic pictures the police had shown her, the Klaw hearings and the graphic words of the stalker's letters. Tears of shame slid down her face.

Don't believe—

"Stop." Bettie made sure she spoke only in her mind to me. "Stop talking. Leave me alone."

Her rejection punched me with a fist of energy. The force hit me so hard that I started to leave her body. I clung, I grasped, I tried to hook into her psyche, I tried everything I could think of to stay inside of her. She flung negative energy at me, fighting me with the strength of a warrior. I fought back, but I felt my strength leaving me. Then I felt another, more familiar energy pulling me out, and I heard, "Aphrodite, you have to leave her."

It was Zeus. I released my hold on Bettie and left her mortal body.

We hovered above the church scene. I looked down on Bettie. She clutched the Bible to her heart and her body shook with her sobs.

"I can't leave her like this. Look how fragile she is, what she believes—"

"What SHE believes. You know the rules. Your archetype doesn't fit anymore. You are rubbing against her free-will," said Zeus.

"You really got attached to this mortal." I jumped at the new voice and turned to see Athena appear beside me.

"I loved her joy. Her happiness and love of life." I pointed down at Bettie. "I don't want to leave her like this—sad, ashamed and guilty. This isn't really her." I could feel Zeus tighten his hold on me, as if afraid I would defy him and return to Bettie.

"She wants to become a warrior," said Athena. She put a friendly arm around my shoulder and joked, "so does this mean I won?"

"Did anyone win?" I asked. I couldn't joke; my heart was broken. I knew the rules that Zeus laid down, but I'd never been pushed out of a mortal by their rejection. In the past, I'd left their body at the time of their death.

I turned towards Zeus. "What happened? What was that third voice I heard directing her towards the church?"

"I can't be sure, but I think it was the modern God," he said. "I heard it once myself. It was when I inhabited Constantine the Great. The Roman Army was in Gaul, and we were just about to set back towards Rome."

Zeus started to raise us up, back towards Mt. Olympus. I watched Bettie grow smaller and smaller as he continued his story. "Suddenly, in front of Constantine and his entire army, a cross appeared in the sky and written below it, in Greek, was *en toutoi ika*—'in this sign, conquer.' I heard a third voice enter Constantine's head at that moment and read the command."

"What did you do?" I asked.

"I got pushed out, just like what happened to you. It was just much harder for me because I hung on to him so tightly and didn't have anyone pulling me out from the other side. I got pretty beat up, and it took me some time to regain my strength. I made the rule after that incident. It isn't possible to stay inside a mortal if you aren't wanted. Free will is the strongest force of a mortal. I thought it might make the exit easier if you thought it was my decree."

"What's going to happen to her?" I asked as we arrived at Mt. Olympus. I hesitated at the entrance, unwilling to face the barrage of questions I knew would greet my return.

Zeus shrugged. "That's up to her. You can watch, if you want, but you can't intervene." He and Athena looked at me, waiting to hear my decision.

"I don't think I'll watch. I prefer to remember as her happy, sexy self that I had the chance to inhabit. I just hope that, maybe we made a difference. I hope that America will remember Bettie Page as a symbol of sexual freedom and joy."

It took decades, but in the 1980s, images of Bettie became popular again. Her fans searched far and wide for her and eventually one discovered her living a quiet life outside of Los Angeles.

After over a year of exchanging letters, Bettie finally agreed to an interview for a biography, but she insisted that no photographs be taken of her.

"I want people to remember me the way I was," she explained.

During the interview, Bettie was asked how it felt to be a mythic symbol of sexuality. She laughed and said, "I haven't the foggiest notion why I'm so popular."

Now you know.

THE END

Kimberly Us is an author and speaker. She writes about strong women, midcentury America, nature, and mythology. Her blog is KimberlyUs.com. A science and English teacher for over twenty-five years, Kimberly infuses her writing with scholarship and entertaining insights. When not reading or hiking, she can be found on the ballroom dance floor. Kimberly lives in Southern California with her husband and two children.